GW00730461

Rose of England

Rose of England

Hilda Lewis

HUTCHINSON OF LONDON

Hutchinson & Co (Publishers) Ltd
3 Fitzroy Square, London W1

London Melbourne Sydney Auckland
Wellington Johannesburg and agencies
throughout the world

First published 1977
© The Executors of Hilda Lewis 1977

Set in Monotype Bembo

Printed in Great Britain by
The Anchor Press Ltd and bound by
Wm Brendon & Son Ltd
both of Tiptree, Essex

ISBN 0 09 129090 2

For Sophie

Chapter One

The marriage of Henry VII and Elizabeth of York, daughter of Edward IV, had been made to please England, and to strengthen the new untried Tudor blood with the true Plantagenet blood royal. Henry's purpose had been to breed sons and safeguard his crown. Elizabeth had accepted her destiny at first unwilling – the man was a usurper and could scarce be considered royal; but he wore the crown and he was comely and kindly.

They had come to care for each other with a deep and tried affection and they were well matched. His brain was cool and needle-sharp; in matters of policy she could not advise him and would not have presumed. But she was a good judge of people, and her graciousness, her real kindliness and clean common sense helped to smooth his difficult path. His happiness she doubled, his sorrows lightened.

Their eldest child Arthur had come hard upon their marriage; he had been premature by a month and was somewhat delicate. Still, he seemed to grow in strength and promised to make a fine man. His looks were handsome, his heart kind and his disposition strong for justice. Named for that legendary king the Tudors claimed for ancestor, he was the stuff of kings.

For nigh on two years there was no sign of a second child and the King was troubled. His mind was set at rest when in May of the year 1489 his Queen was once more with child. In November, when she gave birth to a girl, he was disappointed, but not for long. A girl is not to be despised; one can use her in the game of policies. On the whole he was glad of this child who was named for his mother, Margaret.

7

His second son was born in April 1491 and christened Henry. The following year saw the birth of another daughter. 'Two sons and two daughters,' Henry said. 'The tally's even, we'll not keep it so. I must have more sons.'

For nearly four years there were no more children. But now the baby Elizabeth was smitten by the dreaded wasting disease and died. It was then that some of the brightness tarnished in the Queen. Henry was sorrowful; he, too, loved his children. But he and his wife were young and there was still time.

The next year the Queen was pregnant again. She went into the usual month's retirement before the birth. The great silver font in which all royal infants had been christened was brought from Canterbury, and the King planned especial rejoicings, more public prayers than usual upon such occasions, more alms, more feasting, more wine flowing in the streets.

'It will be a third son. In the old tales the third son is aye the best, aye the luckiest.'

It was, however, another girl. Henry thrust down his disappointment, and once more he was soon over it. All his children were comely, but this last little one was lovely. She had inherited the golden looks of her great-grandmother, Catherine the Fair, Princess of France; but her beauty, though startling, was cast in a gentle mould. Nor did her looks belie her. Like Arthur, Mary was amiable; unlike Margaret and Henry, she was biddable; and so sweet and taking her manner, it added to one's own happiness to give her whatever she might ask.

Margaret and Henry were cut from one piece; they were too alike even to be friends. Proud children, they had from early childhood recognized their high positions; their carriage was imperious though they could be and, indeed, often were gracious. They were both inclined to count, to guard and increase their possessions; they would argue and quarrel were it but the question of a silver pin. Yet Henry could be generous, at times even wildly so; though he often regretted his generosity and would try by hook or by crook to get back the thing

8

he had given away – a habit not to be outgrown with childhood. Margaret could be generous, too, but she would consider with care before giving. When against their will they must surrender some treasure, he would show anger in the reddening of his eyes and the buttoning of his small mouth; she would not betray her unwillingness, but would acquiesce, and, though she might not forget the matter, unlike her brother she bore no grudge.

Mary in her giving was incalculable. If required to part with some cherished thing she might cry and refuse; her desire to keep it being dictated by appreciation of its beauty rather than by desire to possess. But that same appreciation would drive her to offer the thing she loved because it was pretty and she wished someone she loved or pitied to have it.

Arthur the children seldom saw; he had his own lodgings in the King's Side at the Palace of Westminster. Soon he was to be sent to Ludlow with his own Council, his bishops, his high officials and all the great household of a Prince of Wales, there to hold court. Already he was learning something of kingship from his father; soon he would be learning for himself. Two things he had already grasped, the first from his father – the principle of justice; the second his father had never understood and never would – how to gain the love of the people.

The three younger children, Margaret, Henry and Mary, lived in the nursery palace of Eltham in Kent; Westminster was too busy, too noisy, too crowded, too vexed with mists from the river to be suitable for children.

From the time Mary was old enough to understand anything she knew that her father was *King* and her mother *Queen*. What that meant she did not for a long time understand though she knew it was something important that set them apart. *King* and *Queen* were what everyone called them; the children at Eltham also called them *Father* and *Mother*. At first Mary had taken Lady Guildford, who was governor to the two girls, to be their mother. She it was that looked to their

9

well-being, supervised their food, their clothes and their manners. She sat in at Margaret's lessons and guided the steps of the two-year-old Mary.

Mary was still but two when a baby brother was born. For Edmund, third son of the King, there was great joy throughout the land. Oxen were roasted whole, there were fireworks, there was bell-ringing in every village and the churches were loud in thanksgiving.

When Edmund was a year old he was brought with his nurses to Eltham. His mother came with him to see her other children and to rest awhile in the sweet country air; each pregnancy had taken payment of a body that had never been robust.

When the Queen left Eltham, Mary, though sorry, missed her not at all; she had no real part in their lives. But Mary was glad that the baby was left behind; he was better than any plaything. He could laugh and he could cry; he would reach out with tiny hands to come to her, he could kick and he could pull her hair. She hoped he would never grow up.

Things went on gently in the nursery palace under the loving care of Lady Guildford. Margaret learned Latin and French along with Henry. Mary, as yet, was too small to learn, but she sat in with them and listened. Henry was quick at languages. He spoke French well, though he did not like the French people. *France belongs to us; they should speak English!* He said that often. But Latin was quite another matter. He could speak Latin as a bird sings. 'It will be useful because I've to be Pope one day – my father says so.' He was boasting; it was a way he had. 'Arthur will wear one crown, and Margaret another,' for already there was talk of her betrothal to James IV of Scotland. 'And poppet here shall have a crown, too, if she behaves herself!' And he nodded at Mary. 'As for me, I shall wear three crowns and everyone in Christendom will have to obey me, because the Pope speaks with the voice of God!'

All three children had an inborn love of music; they listened with pleasure and they each played an instrument well enough for their years. Henry's talent was indeed a startling one; the nine-year-old played well upon regals, clavichord and lute. Their father was no musician; it was from their mother that they inherited their understanding and their skills. The Queen had been a noted performer until childbearing and other royal duties had put an end to her skill, though not to her understanding.

It was on Mary's fourth birthday that both Father and Mother came to Eltham. They had brought her a very special present. 'It was made for you!' Father said, and put the little lute into her hands. It was very pretty, the wood rich and shining, and inlaid with mother-of-pearl.

Her right hand went out, longing yet not daring to touch the strings. He laughed and bade her play for him; so she picked out a little tune Henry had made for her. 'Bravo!' her father said. He had been pleased, too, with Henry's tune. Henry was always whistling tunes that came from inside his head; and he could play them on any instrument you gave him. Moreover, he could set down the notes with a quill so that they remained for ever for anyone to play. That was, to Mary, the greatest wonder of all.

Upon occasion the children went splendidly gowned, but they were taught to have a care of their clothes. There were many to say that the King was a mean man. The servants whispered it behind their hands; yet they had only to consider their own condition – their decent liveries warm in winter and their good, simple food – to know this was not true. He was not mean, but careful; he had to be – a poor man in a poor country; a man with a great sense of majesty. So, when no visitor was expected, the children put off their velvets to play in frieze or linen. Mary rejoiced in the freedom, but Margaret and Henry disliked this tarnishing of their glory.

At Eltham it was not all pleasant lessons and freedom to play; there was training in the rigid etiquette of the court, for so new a King must hold fast to old courtesies. From the moment the children could stand firm upon their feet they were instructed as to their behaviour. The three curtseys, one at the door, one in the middle of the room and the last at the feet of the King; and there they must kneel and go on kneeling, still as images, until they were given the nod to rise.

The year that Mary was four was a very important year, my lady Guildford said. Fifteen hundred: the beginning of a new century. To Mary it seemed a year like any other – the same lessons, the reading, the writing, the cyphering; but now she sat with the older ones when they learned their Latin and French. And that year Mary had not only her little lute but her first pony and her first hawk; so perhaps 1500 was important, after all. When Henry practised with sword or lance or bow, the two girls would sit with their sewing while Lady Guildford told them tales of the saints, or the more seemly tales of Master Chaucer. There was no one to touch Margaret in the choosing of colours; she could set one against another. Colours you'd never think would be right together, yet you could see at once they were perfect. And her stitches were so fine, so exact, it was as though flowers and creatures grew into life beneath her needle. When Mary stitched there were spots of blood upon her work and her fingertips. Once Lady Guildford found her crying over the spotted work. 'Of course, the Lady Margaret is more skilled than you: she is eleven years old and you but four!' And when Mary wept that she would never understand Latin and French like the others, nor play an instrument with such skill, Lady Guildford said, 'Of course Latin and French do not come easy as yet; the Prince is five years older than you, and that is more than twice your age. As for their instruments, they play well enough, but you have a touch they'll never have. And neither will dance as well as you will, one of these days.'

In the late spring of that year a most distinguished visitor came to Eltham. Dr Erasmus from Holland was already a famous man and it was an honour for princes, even, to receive him. He was staying at Lord Mountford's place nearby, and Master Thomas More brought him over. Dr Erasmus was thirty-four, even to Margaret a great age; and he carried himself with so grave an air as to seem old indeed. They liked Master More better; he was a law student, following in his father's footsteps. He was old, too, as old as twenty-two, but even to Mary he seemed young; he was gay and he moved quickly and made the children laugh.

Lord Mountford had sent warning of the visitors and Lady Guildford, who knew what was due to Dr Erasmus, saw to it that the children were ready to receive him. There they stood in their best clothes in the Great Hall, the household in order of degree assembled about them. Mary remembered that visit very well; but to refresh her memory of it there was the letter Dr Erasmus wrote home of which Master Thomas – one eye already on history – had taken a copy.

. . . The princely children were assembled in the hall and were surrounded by their household. In the middle of the circle stood Prince Henry, then only nine years old. He bore in his countenance a look of high rank and an expression of royalty, yet open and courteous. On his right hand stood the Princess Margaret, a child of eleven years . . . on the other side was the Princess Mary, a lovely lively child, while Edmund, an infant, was held in his nurse's arms.

He talked to the children in Latin. Henry answered easily and quickly; Margaret more slowly but correctly, Mary not at all except by a brilliant smile. She let the wearisome talk flow over her head, but once she fingered the lute hidden in the folds of her gown – she never could be parted from it for long. It let out a *plang* loud as a pistol-shot, at which my lady frowned. Dr Erasmus started, Thomas More laughed, and the cause of it all stood frozen with horror. Master Thomas, laughing still, begged the small girl to play upon the hidden lute; and, Lady Guildford assenting, she played one of Henry's little songs, lifting her small pipe to the words. Then, with that unconscious graciousness of hers, she held out the lute to Master Thomas; and, he playing a little tune, she lifted her skirts and danced.

Those were happy days at Eltham. Summer seemed always bright in its rooms and gardens until the cloud fell and for a while blotted out the sun.

Chapter Two

In London the plague was raging and likely to spread. To escape it and to give the Queen a rest and a change of scene, since she was not fully recovered from the birth of Edmund, the King took his wife and the three older children from Eltham to his loyal town of Calais. Arthur remained in Ludlow; there was little danger of the plague spreading that far and he had his princely duties. Edmund, not yet two, was thought too small to travel.

Mary had never seen the sea before; now she was actually to travel upon it. Now she would set foot in her father's famous town of Calais; an English town in a foreign country where most of the people spoke the French tongue.

Calais went mad with joy to see its King and the three royal children, so handsome and debonair. It hung out its garlands and welcomed them with music and festivities. Mary had a new gown of green velvet edged with purple tinsel, a gown of crimson velvet and one, sea-blue, which she liked more than the others. Her best gown was of black velvet furred with ermine, which, though it set off the ravishing colour of rose and white skin and her bright curls, she did not like at all; black is for dead people, she said.

Towards Calais rode Philip, Archduke of Austria, and Juana his wife, heiress to the Kingdom of Castile. They were the real reasons for the Calais visit. They were all to come together to confirm one betrothal – that of Prince Arthur and the Princess Catherine, daughter of Ferdinand and Isabella of Aragon and sister to this same Juana – and to discuss another, a quite new one, between the little Mary and Charles, Prince of Castile, Infante of Spain, the son of Philip and Juana. Outside Calais, at St Peter's Church, the King of England and the Archduke met, for Philip, notwithstanding his smiling friendship, had no intention of finding himself shut within an English fortress.

The church had been transformed into a dining-chamber of splendour with rich tapestries and gold plate. And the feast matched it in sumptuousness. The children counted the oxen and the young kids, and the great spits set up for their roasting. They watched the wagons unload venison, pasties, spiced cakes and strawberries; they counted seven wagon-loads of cherries. The children were allowed to come in at the end of the feast, for the fruit and sweetmeats, and afterwards all three danced with the high nobility of Austria and Burgundy.

Mary having been seen and approved, both betrothals moved steadily forward. Spain and England needed to strengthen themselves against the common enemy – France. Arthur, not yet fourteen years old, was solemnly contracted to a bride some nine months older than himself.

Neither Henry nor his Queen had set eyes on Catherine. That she was a fair Spaniard and pretty they knew; they had seen her picture; and all reports confirmed that she was sweet-tempered, well educated, and one that loved God with all her heart. What more could any man want? Not the boy Arthur, already in love with her picture.

After a most pleasant month in Calais, Henry and his Queen left in much contentment at seeing their son so firmly and honourably betrothed. Though he would never admit it, Henry could not forget that he was but a new King that some still named *Usurper*; while Spain of ancient lineage was fore-most in honour and majesty in Christendom. And now, the promise – spoken but as yet unwritten – of this second betrothal would knit Spain and England in a double knot of marriage.

Even Prince Henry, nine years old, could see the importance of that. 'Now let this fellow that calls himself King of France take warning! France is ours. It belongs to England. And to England it shall come back. When I am Pope I shall see to it!'

Margaret, with a better wisdom, and also because her nose was a little more out of joint, said very sharply, 'My match is more important, because peace between England and Scotland is much more important. And besides, I'd not fancy Madam Juana as a mother-in-law. She has a strange look in her eye.'

But the four-year-old Mary understood as little of the matter as the Infante Charles who lay now in his cradle sucking his thumb.

The children, their heads a little turned by all the recent excitements, came back to Eltham to find the baby Edmund a sick child, wasting of that same illness that had killed the little Elizabeth. Soon he followed his sister to the grave. Mary missed him intolerably; he had been her pet, her plaything. 'They have put him in the ground,' she wept. 'He will never see the sun again.' And she could not easily be comforted.

A little later the Queen came to Eltham to make arrangements for the three children who were left there. Young as she was, Mary needed no warning from Margaret to ask no question about Edmund; her mother's stricken face was sufficient. The two elder children were to return with their mother to London. Henry was to go to the Tower, where he would have his own lodgings, his own household, his own court. Margaret, soon to be sent as a bride to Scotland, was to lodge in the Palace of Westminster so that she might be measured for new gowns and schooled in behaviour proper to a Queen. If Margaret had been proud before, now she carried that golden head of hers as though it already bore a crown.

To advance her in honours pending her betrothal to the Infante of Spain, Mary was to have Eltham as her own establishment. She was to have the full household of a royal princess – ladies-in-waiting, waiting-women, chamberlain, wardrobe-keeper and every high official; she was to have her own resident physician, for like her mother she was not robust. Of this great household she was the lady – though scarce the mistress, for still Lady Guildford took charge.

To Mary the change was more splendid than happy.

Though the great house at Eltham was full of folk and busy with coming and going, life here was lonely for the little girl. There was less freedom too. There were tutors to teach her those things beyond Lady Guildford's skill, though my lady had overall charge of the little girl's education. Now the four-year-old must apply herself to the study of languages, and to Latin in particular, for that was the language understood everywhere. French, too, was important: it was the language of courts and also spoken everywhere. Spanish might wait a little. If before her breeding had been careful, now it was meticulous. She must learn the rigid etiquette of the Spanish court, and especially the confusing business of greeting guests according to name, family and rank. She must learn the dances of courtly Spain, she must improve her skills upon lute and regals.

Yes, Lady Guildford had been right; 1500 was a very special year. But for all that, Mary still cried for Edmund at nights. Even Margaret, with her tart tongue, was a loss; but she longed for Henry, with his kind and merry ways. Well, soon she would be joining them in London. Already the sewing-women were busy about her new gowns – not that they were exactly new; they had been Margaret's but they were as good as new. They were being taken in at the seams and up at the hem. It was now mid-September 1501, and Catherine, the Princess of Aragon, would soon be here; already she had sailed from Corunna.

'She is coming from a country where the sun shines; what will she think of England?' Mary asked Lady Guildford, eyes upon the falling rain.

'It is not always sunshine in Spain – and it does not always rain here, either.' And, as if to prove my lady's point, the sun burst through suddenly and the rain stopped.

On the fourteenth of November, which is St Erkenwalde's day, Arthur and Catherine were wed. There was a full fort-night of festivities before Arthur took his bride to Ludlow, and it was during this time that the Scottish ambassadors

17

arrived to arrange the marriage between Margaret and King James IV of Scotland. Henry, that wise man, had long desired the match; it should call halt to the bloody border-raids and bless both countries with peace.

Scarcely had the New Year come in than Margaret, too, was married by proxy, on the twenty-fourth of January 1502. The rejoicings lasted a lesser time than for the marriage of the heir to the throne, but still went on for several days. There were jousts and feasts; and, for the poor, cakes and ale and dancing round bonfires.

Yet that year of 1502 was to bring them all great sorrow. In the first week of April Arthur was dead. Within five months of his marriage, and he not sixteen, he died suddenly before his mother and father could be summoned to take a last farewell.

It was the King's confessor who broke the news to him. At first Henry could make no sense of the tidings, but a little later he said quietly: 'I must go to my wife. There is no way to bear this grief but together.' But when he told her, his head understanding but not yet his heart, he found she had already heard; news travels fast in a palace.

From Ludlow came a Catherine very different from the young bride that had gone thither in such high happiness. The mouring procession carrying the embalmed body had joined the King's procession at Worcester. She had seen her young husband buried with great state within the cathedral, and then she had travelled to London with his bereaved parents.

The mother's grief went deeper than the bride's, bitter though that was. Being young another husband could be found for her; certainly she would not be allowed to remain long unwed. But the Queen understood well how shocking and terrible this sudden death must be to the young girl, a stranger in a strange land. At their first meeting in Worcester she had taken the girl into her arms and Catherine had broken into wild weeping; since then she had shed no tear nor spoken scarce a word. Silent, unmoving, she sat in her plain black gown; Elizabeth, for all her desperate longing to know of her son's last hours, asked nothing. In her own good time the girl would speak.

They drove through a black-hung London. London that so short a time ago had been bedecked for the wedding. And now Catherine, lying exhausted in her bed, that same bridal bed at Westminster, found the words pouring forth; and Queen Elizabeth listened closely, for she must miss nothing and the foreign accent made some words hard to catch.

'He was never well; but *never*, Madam! Did you know that?'

Elizabeth did not know. During these past few years she had seen nothing of him. But reports had come regularly from Ludlow; and he himself had never complained.

'Oh, he looked very well . . . at times. A high colour. That colour, Madam, it was a deception. Other times grey; grey as an old man. Yet his courage and his pride were strong. Because he had less strength than other men, he would outride, outrun, outplay them all. For himself he had no pity. I have seen him turn aside and cough; and there would be blood upon his kerchief. He forbade me to tell his physicians; he would take no physic. *A prince must show himself strong*, he said.

'That day . . . three days it was before . . . he died.' She stopped, unable to go on at once. 'He had been playing at the tennis. He was shaking at the end. Fatigue? Fever? Perhaps both. I saw him come within; he had not changed his shirt. It was damp with his sweat. I could not go to him, Madam; I myself had taken the sickness. The fever increased; his little strength grew less; and so he died.'

Henry was not yet Prince of Wales; that title he must not assume until it was certain that Catherine was not with child. For a month she was left to sorrow alone; and then the Queen went straight to the matter.

'But no, Madam, it is not possible. The marriage: it was no proper marriage.'

Not consummated! But the Queen had seen with her own eyes the bride laid naked in her bed to face the coming groom. She had seen her son brought in naked beneath his bedgown, and, that being taken from him, put mother-naked in the bed to face his wife. Now she said, gentle and modest, 'Surely you did together that which is needful and right, and for which marriage is ordained? Surely there was full consummation!'

'Madam, no. He was so weary . . . the marriage and all the festivities. And we were both so shy, Madam. It had been better if, like peasants, we had gone early to our beds. He tried, Madam, he *tried*. But it was useless. He turned from me and he wept. Without a sound he wept, but I knew it. And then he fell asleep. But for me, Madam, I slept not at all, lest he should wake. I know my duty, Madam; I have been taught it well. But a woman must not thrust herself upon a man. So we slept together, apart. Madam, I am a virgin still.'

The King, being male, found the tale hard to believe. And he sent for his son's chamberlain.

'My lord, that wedding-night I myself waited within call, lest I should be wanted. The Prince seemed to me less well than one could wish, especially in a groom. Early next morning, that is, sir, the morning after the marriage, the Prince called for wine; and, being thirsty, called again and again. I said nothing, but then, thinking some comment called for, the Prince, being as the lord King knows, abstemious in his drinking, said all red in the face, "Last night I was in the middle of Spain. Had you been there you had been drier than I!" '

'So much for being a virgin!' the King told his wife later.

'She is indeed virgin!' the Queen said. 'She herself swears it; and she is one whose word is her bond. She would not lie, though it make her Queen of Christendom! Sir, it is no easy matter for a five-month bride to swear her husband never played a husband's part.'

'We have our son's own words!' He had no patience with women's nonsense.

'Repeated months after by a servant . . . and he himself not

20

here to deny it. Consider, my lord, it is not like our son to make a brag of such a thing. The words – if spoken at all – were spoken in shame that he had not played a man's part. I know my son. He is not the first young husband to fail on his wedding-night.'

'And what of the other nights . . . five months of wedded nights?'

'Failure breeds failure. . . . And, besides, he was not well. He thought himself impotent; he would not try again. Sir, I would to God that our daughter Catherine were with child!'

Catherine was not with child. In May Henry was declared Prince of Wales. If he had been proud before, he was still prouder now. Even Margaret, his elder, that was now Scotland's Queen, carried herself before him with a new humility.

Catherine was now Dowager Princess of Wales; and young and forlorn she looked to bear the weight of so sombre a title. She dressed very plainly and had no heart for gay occasions. She kept no court but lived in lodgings fitted to her state, wherever the court might be; and it was well she did so, for the King kept her short of money; often she had not enough to pay her servants.

The Queen was, as always, kind but now she seemed somewhat withdrawn, and not to Catherine alone. 'We are young enough,' she had said the day she heard of Arthur's death, and in June of this year proved her words: she was once more with child.

The year moved on. The Queen's pregnancy was clear to all and she did not look well. Mary, still at court, had been told of the coming child and was overcome with jealousy. Since the death of Edmund two years ago she had been the cherished child. That another should take her place did not suit her at all; moreover, her mother's looks frightened her a little. She did not like the colour of her face; it looked as though it had been smeared with ash.

'The child is restless and unhappy. You had best take her home,' the Queen told Lady Guildford. 'She shall come again for Christmas.'

The New Year of 1503 came in. It was to prove a sadder year even than the last.

The baby was expected in February and the Queen had chosen the Tower for her lying-in. The palace was cheerful enough in summer, but in winter, with its trees, walls and towers often shrouded in mist, it could be very dismal. And surely to the Queen the place must have brought the saddest memories. Here her uncle Clarence had been done to death, and in this same Tower her young brothers had been imprisoned and thereafter no more seen. Why had she chosen this place? Did she hope to bring new life here?

In late January, a full month before the expected birth, the Queen went into seclusion. She stood in the antechamber while her chamberlain cried out, 'The King desires all folk, rich or poor, humble or of great estate, to pray God send the lady Queen a good hour!' And those that stood listening answered with one voice, 'Amen.'

Then she entered the bedchamber where there stood a fine bed beneath a cloth-of-Estate, the covering embroidered with white roses and red. There was a prie-dieu besides, and a cupboard full of such plate as she might need and every piece of pure gold.

The Lord Chamberlain drew the curtains between the anteroom and the birth chamber and now no man whatever, be he the King himself, might enter, save her physicians, and they only at need. Now it was for the women to take over their duties – her chosen ladies, her waiting-women, the midwives, the rockers and any others that had business therein.

The Queen had misjudged her time, or the babe arrived too soon. On the second day of February the child was born – a girl, to be christened Catherine by the Queen's wish, after her sister the Lady Courtenay.

The Queen lay flushed and restless – a b d i , t e midwives whispered; eased now of her l i c sho 1 be sleeping. Within a few days came the signs of the fatal fever of which many after childbirth died.

Of all this the child Mary knew nothing, save that both she and Margaret were banished from their mother's apartments. Margaret, shocked beyond tears, knew well enough their misfortune, but Mary was bewildered.

There had been rejoicing; she had seen the baby and loved her. Looking with delight upon this small sister, she had forgotten all jealousy. But the child brought no comfort to the King or to the Queen, nor to anyone at all. For the mother died of the fever. On her own birthday she died, the eleventh day of February. She was just thirty-seven.

Her mother was dead, and in Mary's heart there was sorrow and deep fear. She was now old enough to understand something of her loss, of what a mother so gracious, so wise and so kind might be to a daughter.

'Do not grieve so.' Lady Guildford took the passionately weeping child into her arms. 'The Queen knows we shall take good care of her little one. And since she cannot return to us, we must wait in patience until, through the redemption of Jesus Christ, we shall go to her.'

So Mary dried her eyes and was a little comforted, even though the baby soon followed her mother in death. She was, after all, not seven years old.

Chapter Three

All England mourned the passing of the good Queen, the beautiful, white-rose Queen.

For twelve days her embalmed body lay within the Tower surrounded by wax candles, each as tall as a man. All about the coffin stood the Queen's ladies clad all in black, and at the head her son's young widow. She had been given the place of chief mourner among the women, from respect for her twofold grief. And it was right and proper, for the Queen had loved her as a daughter; and while the Queen lived Catherine had had good cause to love her, for she alone had spoken for Catherine's dignities and rights and had looked to have got her way.

Now, both the Queen and Arthur being dead, the King's economies had resulted in something like persecution of his son's widow. The whole of her dowry had not as yet been paid and her father was demanding the return of his daughter together with such monies, furnishings, jewels and plate as she had brought with her. Ferdinand had good reason to complain. Henry for his part had paid nothing of the incomes due to her as Princess of Wales or as the Dowager Princess; nor had she heard anything more of those castles and towns with which Arthur had endowed her on her wedding-day. She had barely enough to pay her servants and soon would have nothing left at all. She went dressed like some poor tradesman's wife. After her husband's death she had had made a plain black gown which she had worn continually until it was now wearing thin. Although she had been named as chief mourner, the King had made no offer of a new gown, though all the servants had new mourning liveries. But for all that she had found means to honour the dead Queen; she took her place as chief mourner in a rich dress of black velvet. How she had found the money was her own secret, but she no longer wore the jewelled bracelets her husband had given her.

On the twelfth day the coffin, covered with black velvet, was placed in a great open carriage to be borne to Westminster. At the coffin's head a life-sized image sat upon a throne. It was an exact likeness of the Queen in her royal robes, the crown upon her flowing hair, her right hand holding the sceptre. At the four corners of the great chair knelt black-clad ladies in prayer.

Watching from a window this last passing of her mother, Mary caught sight of the seated figure and screamed with terror. This was not her mother; it was a thing that sat, unchangingly poignant in expression, but moving neither lip nor lid. She ran from the window and refused to look again.

The King was a changed man – so folk said. But indeed he was the same man he had always been save that he smiled less and laughed not at all. He went his lonely way, his eye watching affairs in Europe, his shrewd and devious mind turning over policies and considering marriages – for his son, for his daughter Mary, and (in spite of his real grief) for himself, if it should be for the country's good.

Princess Margaret, already wed by proxy, was soon to leave her home and wed her lord in good earnest. Where money must be spent, the frugal Henry could show himself generous, and when she eventually set out from Richmond with her great train, she carried with her to Scotland cloths of gold and silver, velvets, furs, and gold plate, and was attended by above a hundred servants. There rode with her, too, the Earl of Dorset, the Lord of Derby, Constable of England, the Earl of Kent, the Bishops of London and Norwich, and knights and ladies to take her as far as York, and to lead them all, very splendid, the Somerset herald.

Standing in the great gateway between her father and the

Princess Catherine, Mary watched her sister go. Margaret wore that proud look of hers, but at their farewell kiss the child felt a tear upon her cheek; and that tear was not her own. Mary guessed that the new Queen of Scotland was in truth full of fears. 'I do pray God,' she told Lady Guildford, 'she will find a kind lord!' And then, 'I am glad I am too little to marry. Not for all those fine things would I leave my home to sleep in bed with a strange man and have his children!'

'I am glad, too,' my lady said. 'Yet your time will surely come; and when it does you must be ready.' And she looked at Mary with an almost pitying smile.

But it was not Mary whose future the King had been pondering, calculating his moves as on a chess table, at this time. His eldest son was dead, but the young widow so recently a bride, was here under his hand, and he was loth to let her go. England needed the friendship of Spain to stand against a distrusted France, and needed, too, the gold Ferdinand had promised as a wedding-dower. Only half had been paid and now that his son-in-law was dead Ferdinand seemed intent on obtaining, not only the return of this gold, but of his daughter and the rest of the goods she had brought with her. How far was he serious in this demand? Would Ferdinand dare to weaken his alliance with England when he needed her countenance and help against France? Henry felt that Ferdinand dare not quarrel with him at this moment, and, as for himself, he had the girl under his hand and had no intention of paying back one gold piece. Rather he must devise some way to keep it in honour and lay hands upon the rest.

The answer was simple. It was time to remember that he had another son, and betroth the girl to the new Prince of Wales. So the alliance would stand and the unpaid dowry be made good. The little matter of that first marriage, that ugly word incest? The Pope should see to it. In Spain Ferdinand was mulling over the same problem and, ignoring his Queen's bitter opposition, came to the same conclusion.

The two about to be betrothed had no say in the matter. With his widowed daughter-in-law King Henry never thought to exchange a word on the subject, but he did send for his son.

The boy was at first taken aback and then flattered. He liked Catherine. She was pretty, sweet-natured and well educated, as well as good and pious – had all the graces to be looked for in a queen. True, she was six and a half years older than he, but she was so small, so young-looking, and he himself so tall that they looked of a like age. All the same, she was his brother's widow. He had seen them laid naked in the nuptial bed, and at twelve years he was old enough to understand the significance of that!

'Sir, it is against God's law . . .'

'That you must leave to those wiser than yourself. The girl's a virgin. Do you think I would put the succession of my son's son in jeopardy? And do you question the Pope that all good Christian men hold speaks with the voice of God? If he holds this betrothal good, then good it shall be.'

'I would not have Madam Catherine troubled by such an affair. She has troubles enough already.'

'You might put an end to them. Can you like the girl?'

'I like her very well.'

'Then you may leave your conscience in my hands.'

And when the boy would have protested: 'I am your father and your King. It is for me to command; for you to obey.'

Catherine was in her little sitting-room with Mary when she heard the news. These two, both lonely, had been drawing closer in friendship. The eighteen-year-old Dowager Princess of Wales, poor and robbed of her dignities and dowers, found in the seven-year-old child a warmth and understanding that helped to lessen her miseries, while Mary found in her sister, as she called her, a companionship she had never known with Margaret. Catherine, very pretty with her red-gold hair falling in curls and her blue eyes, was gentle and kind. But she was paler than before. She had heard rumours of the intended betrothal and was sick with horror. To wed her to her dead husband's brother! It was a thing forbidden in Holy Writ. It could not be true. Her father would never allow it.

Mary suddenly interrupted their conversation to say, 'Oh, Catherine, you are not well! Is it the fever again?'

'No, it is my head,' and a weary hand went up to push back her hair.

'I'll get you a wet cloth!' Mary ran into the closet to soak her kerchief in water. She was tying it about Catherine's head when Lady Guildford came in.

'Well, well, my young ladies,' she cried out, over-cheerful so that Mary, knowing her ways, guessed at unwelcome tidings.

'There should be an end to fevers and to tears, and to Madam Catherine's cheeseparings also. Everything turns to good, I promise you!'

Catherine's pale face beneath the bandage was white now as the linen itself.

'Yes, Madam Catherine, you are to marry again. And in England. And the groom? The handsomest and highest in the land – and well you know who that shall be! It is all arranged. The lord King will send for you himself at the proper time to give you the news, but I am come to prepare you. All is arranged between your two fathers. You are to wed His Highness the Prince. You shall be in truth Princess of Wales and no dowager, which is more fitting to your age. And in God's good time you shall be Queen of this land.'

'No!' Catherine's voice was horror-stricken. 'It is incest!'

'Madam, keep that thought from your heart and especially from your tongue. What the lord Pope agrees to must be both right and proper. You shall not be betrothed until he, himself, speaks the word.'

'He will not speak it. No man, not even the Pope's self, dare offend against God's law.'

'Madam, I tell you, the Pope will speak in the matter and his answer will be *Yes*. And, Madam; let me warn you! Your father is accounted the wisest man in Christendom save for one only – your father-in-law. In this all Christian men hold them equal. Shall you set yourself against the lord Pope and these two Kings?'

'Can I wed a boy, a child?' Desperate, Catherine seized upon a lesser point that not even the Pope could deny. 'He is scarce twelve. Too young, too young!' And she wrung her hands.

'It is a betrothal now and not a wedding.' Lady Guildford had been well primed. 'Come wedding-time the Prince will be a man in size and wisdom.'

In spite of Catherine's anguished letters to her father, the marriage-treaty was signed. On the twenty-fifth of June, 1503, these two were privately betrothed at Lambeth by the Archbishop himself. Catherine made the responses and accepted the ring as in a dream. She could not believe she was betrothed to her dead husband's brother. And from Rome no dispensation had come, nor did it come in the years that followed, though, as time passed, Catherine herself became agreeable to the match.

Yet, as others warmed to the project, the King of England was himself becoming dubious. There were, after all, marriages which might be even more advantageous to his son, and the dowry was still not paid in full. At least he would sanction no marriage until it was, and continued to keep his daughter-in-law without funds so that she could now no longer feed her servants, hardly even herself, and such luxury as a new gown could not be thought of.

The years were passing, she would be twenty-one by the end of 1506. It was old for a bride, and for a Spanish bride very old indeed. She was beginning to lose her looks, as her own mirror betrayed. Pale to the lips and hollow-eyed she was no longer slender, she was thin. The King, when he looked at her, grew more doubtful about the match than ever, he wanted a healthy wife for his only son. Besides, he had in mind another alliance with Spain more to his liking. There was the long ago unwritten agreement concerning betrothal between his daughter Mary and the Prince of Castile. It would bring him not only friendship with Castile but also with the little Prince's Habsburg relatives. Catherine's marriage with the Prince of

Wales might make that betrothal impossible. The kinship on both sides, involved and troublesome, might well prove an insuperable barrier. The girl must content herself at the moment with her present condition.

But the Prince of Wales, with young chivalry, was yet more drawn to his betrothed. Her piteous looks pulled at his heartstrings; and besides he knew her to be shabbily treated. These days he looked at her with more than a brother's kindness. And while his courtesy and warmth urged her heart towards him, in him the sense of his desire to help the poor young thing – for in her distress and helplessness she seemed younger than himself – quickened kindliness to love.

Chapter Four

Meanwhile, changes had been taking place in and for Mary who now, in 1506, at the age of ten, became for the first time deeply conscious of Charles Brandon, her brother's personal gentleman. Up to the present she had taken him for granted. The two young men went about linked in easy friendship, the arm of one thrown carelessly about the other. They were always together – where one saw Henry, one saw Brandon. It had been so ever since she could remember.

Six years older than the Prince, Brandon was handsome and debonair; he was skilled in the use of any weapon, in sports and games he excelled. He was much like the Prince in looks: they had the same fair and ruddy colouring, the same bone structure in the broad handsome face, the same tall stature, the same graceful carriage. They had the same way of speaking ... almost. The young man had come to court as a small boy, the Suffolk speech broad upon his tongue. Now courtly mode came naturally, save when moved, when his native vowels marked the country boy.

The two might have been taken for brothers; and it was as a brother Brandon had treated Mary, a kindly elder brother. She, however, now felt a new shyness in his presence. She was no longer forward in speaking to him as became her rank; she waited for him to speak, treasuring every word. She watched for his coming with an eagerness she did not feel for Henry's. When he did not come she felt the down-dropping of her heart. When he appeared, her heart leaped; delight, a sweetness flooded her whole body. She had, all unknowing, fallen in love.

At ten, one may feel without understanding. Especially was this so with Mary; her whole life had been a forcing-house of the emotions. She had seen overmuch of death, mourning the loss of her mother, her brothers and the infant she had longed to cherish. She had seen overmuch of betrothals; she had seen the marriage of young Arthur as well as his death . . . life and death enclosed within the short passage of his few years – and she herself had already lived ten of her own. She had seen Margaret, but seven years older than herself, joyfully wed. She had seen her sister-in-law widowed and now again betrothed. Death one may forget, if one is young enough; but betrothals and marriages are in the very air one breathes. She could hardly fail to be impressed by the solemnity and splendour displayed by these high events. Her experiences had gone deeper than Lady Guildford or the child herself understood.

Betrothal and love could, unfortunately, be two different things. Betrothals were to serve the will of one's parents. One might be betrothed to an infant in the cradle, or to a man ancient enough to be a grandfather. Yet it did not always turn out so unlucky: witness Margaret and James, Catherine and Arthur, Catherine and Henry. Betrothals generally ended in marriage, love not always. The duties of marriage she understood. She had pressed Lady Guildford in the matter, and in the atmosphere of such events, my lady could not but explain. The idea of a hateful betrothal for herself never entered Mary's head. It was not possible. To whom she might be betrothed she had no idea; the kind of man she meant to love she knew very well. She had seen debonair gentlemen aplenty and had made her choice. He was the most handsome, the most gallant, the most brave and kindest of them all. Charles Brandon outshone all men, even her brother.

Lady Guildford, as a rule so kind, was a little short in the matter of Master Charles Brandon. She did not care for the child's interest in a man eleven years older than herself and already twice and most disastrously married . . . or if not twice married, twice entangled.

'He is one to seek his own advantage always,' she said. 'He is nothing but the son of a poor esquire; a gentleman, yes; but in no way outstanding or even interesting. Brandon's good fortune came to him from his father's death on Bosworth field. And that your own father, the lord King, saw and remembered. William Brandon was standard-bearer to your father; he was killed pushing his way towards Richard of Gloucester, clearing the road for his master – killed by Richard himself. If a man has to die, what better way to reward him than to benefit his son? In that same battle William Brandon's son and heir was killed; but within a few months his second son was born.'

Mary's eyes filled with tears, picturing the dreadful news coming to the manor house near King's Lynn; the new-made widow bereft of husband and son, and carrying a child already fatherless.

'Mistress Brandon died shortly afterwards and the child's grandmother brought him up,' Lady Guildford went on. 'The King might have been pardoned if he had forgot the whole affair, but he did not forget. For all he was so poor and in need of every penny, he sent Mistress Brandon a sum every year; small but sufficient to bring up her grandson. And when the boy was ten years old, the King, hearing that he was quick-witted, good-looking and well mannered, sent for him and made him page in Prince Arthur's household.

'And there Prince Henry took an instant liking to him and asked for the young man as his own personal gentleman-in-waiting. Fortune has favoured young Brandon. Let us hope he prove worthy of his fortune!'

My lady's tone showed she doubted it. 'Many gentlemen are jealous of his looks. But not the Prince – he's handsomer still.'

He is not. He is not! Mary made her silent passionate protest.

'They are jealous also because of Brandon's skill with weapons, and in sports and games. But there, too, your brother has no need of jealousy. Brandon is better, but he's six years older. In less than that time the Prince will outstrip him and they both know it.'

Mary nodded. That at least was true.

There was silence while Mary thought of Brandon's every perfection.

'My brother loves him' – Lady Guildford was startled for the girl's tone was tender, as though she had said, *I love him* – 'because he's so merry a fellow. He's ready for every jest, ready to laugh, even when the jest goes against himself!'

The Prince has not learned to laugh at himself and never will. The thought was instant to both.

'Meanwhile,' my lady said, grim with her new suspicion, 'as I've said, that young man watches his chances. He knows that in those things which he does better than the Prince he must not shine too bright. He carries himself with care . . .'

'Is that wrong?'

'It depends. It could be right and proper. But Brandon feeds that pride with which the Prince was born, and which his nurture has done nothing to lessen. He flatters . . . he flatters overmuch!'

Chapter Five

The King of England was to entertain the King and Queen of Castile at Windsor. Mary had the first news of this event, so important to herself, from Catherine.

For days now wind and weather had been cruel; the fierce winds and high seas had driven ships off course; some had been driven into harbour, their whereabouts as yet unknown. They might well have been wrecked and none as yet knew their fate. Catherine, especially, was troubled. Her sister with her husband the Archduke Philip were on their way from Castile to the Netherlands to be crowned.

Now Catherine came running into Mary's rooms at Westminster, where she had been staying, flushed and happy and very pretty in spite of thin cheeks and shabby gown.

'My sister, my sister Juana is in England. *In England!* I cannot believe it, yet it is true. The terrible storms we have all been cursing have turned to blessing for me. The wind has driven their ships upon our coast . . . a long way from here, but still in England. A little port in your West Country. Melcombe, they call it. Oh Mary, Mary, I shall see my sister again; after all these long years see her and touch her, my own flesh and blood. Mary, Mary, you cannot imagine my joy!'

It was later that day that Lady Guildford sought out Mary.

'Do you remember, Madam – it is all of six years gone – your journey into Calais?'

Yes, Mary remembered; remembered running upon the beach and being scolded that she did not lift her skirts above salt wetness; and in the ev⸺ ⸺ ⸺ y had dressed her very fine and brought her into the great hall to sing to the ladies and gentlemen, and there had been more cherries than any child could eat.

'Chief among those ladies and gentlemen was the Princess Juana and her husband. Your betrothal to their son was discussed then, agreed upon but never ratified. But now that your father has invited these storm-driven guests to Windsor, I think, Madam, that the question will arise again.'

Betrothed: to a husband six years of age! She, a young lady of ten! And a young lady, moreover, who knew a pretty gentleman when she saw one; had, indeed, seen the prettiest gentleman of them all! A husband of six years old! She began to laugh at the very notion. My lady's face cut short the laughter.

The King had seen the hand of Heaven in this business. It was almost as if God's own breath had driven the visitors upon his shore. He had now determined on a double marriage with Spain: Mary to the young Prince of Castile, which would strengthen relations with Austria through the Archduke Philip, and with Castile through Juana. As for the marriage of the Prince of Wales . . . if Ferdinand paid up handsomely with the dowry, it might go forward. If not, he would betroth the Prince of Wales in France. . . . With Spain, Austria and France linked to him in marriage, he would be in the strongest of positions.

Henry sent his messengers agallop to welcome the visitors; and to bid the gentlemen who lived hard by to attend upon them. Henry also sent horses, litters and servants to convey them into London. The high winds continuing, there was nothing for the unwilling Philip – who knew the dangers of confrontation – to do but to accept the invitation. The King of England was not to be gainsaid.

But Philip would come alone. The Queen of Castile was fatigued with the storm and distressed by reason of the wreck of some of her fleet. She must rest. . . .

Catherine's grief was bitter. She had hoped so much from this meeting; not only because she longed to see her sister, but because she believed it must see the end of all her difficulties. Still, Juana's husband was coming; that was better than nothing.

Sunday, the first of February, 1506. At Windsor in the King's private closet, Catherine and Mary waited. Mary wore a rich gown of Tudor green and white that so became her red-gold hair. Catherine too wore a rich gown – a new one bestowed by the King for the occasion. It was blue and should have become her well, save for her pallor. She wore the Spanish mantilla held by a high jewelled comb. About them stood their ladies, Catherine's making a better show than usual by reason of the King's generosity, if generosity it could be called.

The two Kings came in together, arms linked. Down went all the ladies in their curtseys; Philip raised and kissed the two Princesses. Mary wondered why they called this man 'The Fair'. He was, she supposed, handsome enough in his big fleshy way; but he was neither elegant nor debonair – he was too fat. One look at those cold grey eyes and she knew Catherine's fate. He looked to be a man indifferent to the joys or griefs of others. Poor Catherine! If her fate hung upon him, unless it prove to his own advantage, she'd know little of happiness.

Catherine played her part well. Her manner towards him was perfect; deferential as to a King; affectionate as to a brother.

The next evening there was to be a great entertainment and she had been told that Philip wished to see her dance in the Spanish fashion. She, who had danced so little of late, and the dances of her own country not at all, spent the day practising with her favourite lady, Maria de Salinas. The night of the festivities saw them both in Spanish dress. Catherine's was an evening court gown brought from home and, since she had had few occasions to wear it, new and bright. Her mantilla was held in place by a small golden crown and, to emphasize her virginity, beneath the mantilla the long hair flowed free. Richly dressed, colour high in her cheeks, eyes bright, her looks belied her sad state. She danced with grace but with little vigour; she had just recovered from a bout of fever.

The visitor turned a cold eye upon the pretty performance and languidly clapped. Henry, desirous of showing his daughter's paces, requested her also to dance. He could have chosen no better method. Mary was not only extremely pretty, with her bright blue eyes, her fair curls hanging beneath a cap of pearls, and her childish figure, clothed in green and white, but she was a natural dancer. With enchanting grace she moved now, her small face alight with happiness. She was happy because she loved dancing and because this King was her father's guest; pleasing him, she honoured her father.

All eyes were fixed upon her as she danced alone in the great room; all eyes except one pair. The visitor sat, his face turned aside to talk with his host. Mary's heart burned; yet still she proceeded according to her instructions. Her dance finished, she approached the visitor and invited him to dance with her. She had been unwilling to do this; it was, she thought, scarce proper for a lady to invite a gentleman, unless the lady were a queen. She had said as much to Lady Guildford. 'You take the Queen's place,' my lady had said. 'If it were not proper your father had not asked it.'

Now, she was more unwilling than ever. She did not like this man; but her father must be obeyed.

He turned upon her that same cold eye; and dismissing her as an importunate child, said, 'I am a sailor, not a dancing master,' and turned again to her father.

It was as though he had slapped her in the face. She bit upon her jaw to hide its trembling. She felt her mortification because she was a child; because she was, tonight, taking her dead mother's place; she was doing her best and she had failed. She rose from her curtsey and went to sit by Catherine at the end of the dais. She sat there and wished herself dead.

She was not to be left in peace long. Her father ̶ ̶ ̶ her to show her skill upon some instrument. Obedient, she sent for her lute and played a little song to which King Philip did not pretend to listen; again he lifted languid hands in applause. She played next upon the clavichord; he lifted his languid hands again. Nothing it seemed would please him.

But indeed he meant nothing to please him. He was here against his will.

She had her reward that night when her father sent for her. 'Daughter,' he said, 'you have acquitted yourself well; and so says everyone. Nor was it easy for you. You carried yourself not like a child but like a queen. I am proud of my daughter this day!' And he smiled one of the old kind smiles so rare in him since her mother died.

King Philip remained at Windsor until his Queen arrived some few days later. Mary liked her even less than she liked Philip. Juana was as unlike the gentle fair Catherine as any sister could be. She was handsome in a fierce dark Spanish way; and she was very proud, as though she owned the world. Queen in her own right, believing that no blood in Christendom equalled the royal blood of Spain, she did not deign to despise England and its King: she simply thought them beneath her notice and did not trouble to hide her indifference. When she spoke she scarce looked at the one to whom she spoke – be it the King himself or the child who might marry her son. Her eyes moved only with Philip. When he was absent she was gloomy; she did not answer when spoken to; it was doubtful, even, that she heard. She did not speak at all save to rebuke. Mary did not wish for her as a mother-in-law, even had her son been as desirable as could be, and not merely a child of six.

Catherine too got no pleasure from this once loved, once longed-for sister.

But for all Juana's daunting behaviour, Henry found – or appeared to find – her attractive. No woman ever daunted him, and no woman he ever loved, save his Queen . . . and that only by slow degrees. And though, even shortly after her death, he considered this marriage and that, calculating, as it

39

were mathematically, the possible advantages of each, he never put another woman in his wife's place.

Within a day or two the court left Windsor for Richmond; and there, with great display, King Henry entertained his guests with tournaments and sports, with feasts and dances.

'A treaty has been made between the lord King your father and his guests,' Lady Guildford said.

Mary's cheeks whitened. There was a question she dared not ask; her eyes asked it for her.

'There's been no talk of betrothal; nor can be . . . yet. A treaty of friendship and commerce only. It cannot at the moment be otherwise. The Prince is already betrothed to the Princess Claude of France.'

Mary let out her breath in a sigh of relief.

'Do not rejoice too soon,' my lady warned. 'Betrothals have been broken before this. And will be again, I make no doubt France and Spain are both untrustworthy when it comes to their own interests!' She might have added, *Like England, and every Christian country*.

Lady Guildford was right. There was no word of a treaty of betrothal between Mary and Charles of Castile. And she was right on another matter also. A betrothal may be broken.

Louis of France was not content with the betrothal of his daughter, the Princess Claude, to the Prince of Castile. The marriage treaty provided that several rich provinces of France, including Brittany, should be part of the wedding dowry. To gain Brittany he had put away his good wife, Jeanne, who had been gentle and ever blind to his infidelities. True, being plain and lame, she had need of such virtues, but to have married in exchange that hard piece Anne of Brittany for the sake of her inheritance, and then to give away Brittany with both hands? And not Brittany alone. Spain had covetous eyes on Normandy and Guienne. What sort of bargain was that?

A betrothal may be broken. . . . Could England, by any means, break the betrothal between the daughter of France and the

40

son of Spanish Juana and Austrian Philip? For if that betrothal were honoured, then, against the power of Austria, France, Castile and very likely all Spain, England stood alone.

If ever the King of England prayed, it was now. And his prayers were answered.

Suddenly, without any warning, the Princess Claude was betrothed to her father's cousin, Francis of Angoulême, heir apparent to the throne of France.

Now it was the turn of Juana and Philip to be outraged. And with them the young Prince's grandfather, the Emperor Maximilian. This was the second time a royal Habsburg had been so insulted by France: first his daughter Margaret, now his grandson. The Archduchess Margaret said nothing, she was one to bide her time.

Henry was jubilant. Once more confidential messengers crossed and recrossed the sea. Once more letters went backwards and forwards between Spain and England, England and Austria.

Chapter Six

Negotiations were in hand in the matter of the match between the Prince of Castile and the Princess of England. Now it was Mary's turn to pray, and her prayers were answered, shockingly answered.

Philip, Archduke of Austria and King of Castile, that sturdy man, suddenly died. Poison? A chill? A heart attack? Rumours ran everywhere about Christendom. Juana asked no question, listened to no rumour, slipping deeper into madness. Her husband was not dead. They had put him in a coffin because they were insane; the whole world was insane except herself!

Now Henry of England must reconsider his plans. Earlier he had been pursuing the Archduchess Margaret. Vows of love, letters enclosed with marriage treaties had flown from England to the Netherlands. *Never let go till the bird is safe in the hand* was one of Henry's maxims, and *a wise man keeps several strings to his bow* was another.

Of late, it had been in his mind to marry his son's widow himself. He could then, without question, keep that part of her dowry already in his hands, and ask for a great deal more. And Spain would pay. Now he fitted a third string to his bow. He would marry Juana, get his hands on Castile and with it Spanish trade. Also the Queen's priceless dower – she was very, very rich.

That might mean some reshuffling of his plans. He would marry the Prince of Wales to the Princess Claude of France, thus breaking her betrothal to the Count of Angoulême. Charles, Juana's son, could then be betrothed to Mary according to the unwritten agreement. A splendid arrangement to knot England, France, Austria and Castile into one family. The problem of blood kinship would present some difficulties, but that was a matter for the Pope.

Henry made his offer for Juana more favourable and tempting even than those with which he had wooed the Archduchess.

The offer was refused. Ferdinand of Castile had been appointed regent for the mad Juana. He had no intention of letting Castile slip into Henry of England's grasp. Madam the Queen of Castile was not well enough, at present, to consider any offer of marriage.

'Not well enough . . . at present!' an angry King of England told young Wolsey, his chaplain, as clever a young man as ever stepped. 'She's well enough, I warrant you – aye, and young enough to bear children!' And that, since he had now but one son, was an added attraction. When his tirade ended, Wolsey spoke softly, compassionately.

'Sir, the lady is *mad*!'

So Henry must forgo his fine match. He must busy himself once again with matchmaking: press forward with the betrothal of Mary and the little Prince of Castile, and address himself, with even more passion, to the Archduchess Margaret, still more desirable since she had been named guardian to the unfortunate Charles whose father was dead and whose mother was mad.

Life had indeed changed for the little boy. Now his two grandfathers were to act as his regents: Ferdinand, King of Aragon would rule for Juana in Castile; the Emperor Maximilian, ruler of the Netherlands, Burgundy and much else besides, would be responsible for the boy's Habsburg possessions and for his upbringing. And since he was so busy a man and his interests so widespread, he appointed his daughter to be Regent of the Netherlands, to protect the boy's rights there; the child himself was to be brought up in her court at Lille.

Margaret, Archduchess of Austria and Savoy, had always a finger to stir in every pot in Christendom. Now, powerful Regent of the Netherlands, she could use her whole hand. Her father trusted her political acumen, as well he might; in affairs of the heart she was not so fortunate. She was now twenty-eight and at the height of her beauty. She had been twice married and twice widowed. At seventeen she had married John of Aragon; a few months later he was dead. She was twenty when she married Philibert, Duke of Savoy; within two years he also was dead. She might have been Queen of England, for Henry pursued and went on pursuing. She refused; and went on refusing. But all the time she played at acceptance, she and her father offering friendship, professing to consider his proposals and treaties. And if he would show himself the enemy of France, how much more than friendship might be offered?

She had her own score against France. Neither she nor her father could forget the insult France had offered them. She had been taken from her home at two years of age to be brought up at the French court, as the bride of the Dauphin – Madame la Dauphine, future Queen of France. And then, quite suddenly, at fourteen, she had been packed off home again, humiliated to the point of disgrace; and her betrothed, who had become King Charles VIII of France, had married the heiress of Brittany to add her inheritance to his own.

Sent packing after twelve years, and by then of marriageable age, she had had to learn her native tongue and her native ways afresh. She, the adulated and adored, who took precedence of all, had been, without warning, jilted, discarded. The shock to the girl was tremendous, her humiliation deep. France had no greater enemy. Now she worked and would never cease to work for the downfall of France.

Now the insult had been repeated . . . in exactly the same circumstances. Her nephew Charles's match had been unceremoniously broken. Princess Claude had been betrothed in France; once more a Habsburg had been insulted. Now Margaret had her chance to make France tremble with the

English-Spanish-Habsburg match. It was she who reopened the old negotiations that pushed on the betrothal of Mary and Charles.

Mary's blood ran chill. She prayed night and day that the Blessed Virgin would not permit her to be married to the son of the mad-woman. Now it was not so much that the Prince of Castile was too young – certainly the years would amend that. He was the son of the mad-woman, and nothing could alter that.

Lady Guildford kept her informed as to how matters stood.

'They are to meet at Calais; your father the King and his Council are to discuss with Madam the Archduchess Margaret the question of your marriage.'

But the meeting did not take place. The King fell ill. Mary's heart lightened a little at the respite.

'A not inconvenient sickness,' her brother Henry said. 'He needs time to think. He does not know what to make of this sudden haste for the Spanish match. He does not trust the Archduchess, and with reason. Under that pretty face of hers, she's steel; a man's brains, so they say. God keep us all from women of steel, and even more from women with brains!'

But King Henry from his sickbed – if, indeed it were a sickbed – asked that his commissioners and those of the Archduchess meet at Calais to discuss business arrangements 'and other pleasant and comfortable matters'.

King Henry's suggestion was acceptable. In the autumn of 1507 commissioners from both sides met at Calais. Towards the end of December the terms of the marriage contract were agreed.

The King sent for his daughter to make this known to her, but she knew already. Lady Guildford had prepared the girl lest she show her distress. Henry received her in the Presence Chamber, the Prince of Wales at his right hand, his Council all about him. He knew his daughter's mind in the matter of the Spanish marriage and was making it clear that her behaviour must fit this most solemn occasion.

Mary thought, as she made her low curtsey at the door, how tired he looked, how old! Nor, as she made her halfway curtsey, did she see reason to change her opinion. Her third curtsey brought her to the King's feet. He motioned to her to rise and she stood with hands clasped and head bowed, as became a young daughter before her father; the more so when that father was a King.

'Daughter,' he said, 'your marriage is arranged. At Easter, God willing, the Emperor's ambassadors will arrive, and you shall be wedded by proxy to the Prince of Castile. You will hold yourself to be his true wife. Yet you must be patient; he is but seven years old. Well, you are young enough to wait, and it will be worth the waiting! One day you shall be the wife of the Emperor, of the ruler of Austria, Burgundy and the Low Countries, and of more towns and islands than I can well name!'

She had been prepared for this and had learned her lesson well. With a quiet face she made her curtsey and uttered the required words: 'It shall be as it please the lord King my father.'

'The Lady Guildford will tell you all you need to know so that you may carry yourself as shall best stand with our honour and our pleasure.' Then, knowing her feelings and fearing lest they break through to the discomfiture of all concerned, especially the Habsburgs, he added, very kind, 'You have our permission to withdraw.' So, she reversed her curtseys and was glad indeed to find herself on the other side of the door. And now, blinded by tears and regardless of any who might see, she gathered up her gown and ran to the safety of her own rooms and the comfort of Lady Guildford.

'Madam,' she began, 'oh Madam!' And at the sight of her tear-stained face my lady, well knowing that her charge's thoughts were fixed only on Charles Brandon, spoke freely, without the caution she had intended. 'Oh Mary, sweetheart, it is useless to weep. Waste no more thoughts upon a man who is not worthy of you! Neither you nor he is free. Sweetheart, he is *wed*; had been indeed twice wed. And both wives living!'

Lady Guildford went on. 'The story of his marriages do not make pleasant telling. It is but two years ago that he stole Mistress Anne Browne from her father's house and got her with child. He contracted marriage with her, so she says. But what proof? No priest, no one to stand for witness. What shall Mistress Anne do now, she and her bastard child? That same year he repudiated the marriage . . .'

Mary knew the tale; it had been common gossip at court. 'He could not if it were legal.'

'It is easy enough to break through such a marriage,' my lady said. 'A young and ignorant girl; and no one able to find the priest who married them . . .'

'He will make full amends.' Mary would hear nothing against her love.

'Can one make full amends for so much shame and suffering? He meant to better himself; that is always his way! That same year, his marriage made and repudiated, he took to himself another wife, and a vastly wealthy one.'

Mary did not need telling about Margaret, a Neville by birth and widow of Sir John Mortimer. Twenty years older than Brandon, she was not only a very great heiress but a very great shrew. Yes, Mary had known the stab of jealousy on her account, too.

'This time, too, he chose a wife from whom it was easy to break free. He spent a good deal of her money and then got rid of her; but not until he'd claimed and won, as her husband, mind you, a goodly slice of her Mortimer inheritance. She was easy enough to be rid of . . . too near in blood to his first wife. The Church declared it no marriage. And now, they say, he's to wed his first love again in full court.'

'She's not his love!' Mary was stubborn.

'Then why wed her again? Madam, I beg you, put all thought of Brandon from your mind. You are eleven and innocent; were he as chaste as the moon itself, he is not in your stars. You are royal Tudor – and he a simple esquire. Of the matter of your own betrothal I do not speak.'

'I am sick to death of Brandon's marriages!' Mary said.

'But whatever folk say, whatever he himself appears to have done, he is a true gentleman and to that I'll hold to my dying day. As to the matter of my betrothal – there is no treaty signed as yet; talk, talk, merely.'

The New Year of 1508 came in with great rejoicing . . . to all but Mary. In February the betrothal treaty was signed. Mary carried herself as was expected; she said the right words, smiled her gracious smiles, made a show of content. The King sent letters to the Lord Mayor of London and to the mayors of every town to tell them of the great and honourable marriage treaty now concluded. By marriage of one daughter to the King of Scots and the other to the Prince of Castile England was safe from all enemies. The whole country showed its joy.

That spring Mary had further cause for grief. Charles Brandon married Anne Browne in full court with festival and song. The thought of this marriage, the happy groom and bride – for surely Brandon must love his Anne – and her own barren betrothal, filled the girl with an aching misery she could scarcely endure. Nor was her misery the less that within a few months the happy Anne was again – and proudly – pregnant.

Spring wore on and it was June. By the great preparations to entertain the ambassadors that should come to see her wed, by the fitting of new gowns and the display of jewels she should carry with her, Mary could no longer doubt but that the marriage must take place. She could hope for nothing now save one thing. She wanted Brandon to know that when she herself departed for Flanders she left her heart behind in England. And one more thing: that he might think of her at times, and not as a sister.

She wandered alone in the summer gardens at Richmond. There was a clipped yew alley, very dark, and, walking slow and sad within it, she did not see the shadowy shape moving towards her until it thickened – and there stood her heart's love. She took his appearance as a gift from a kindly god. She stood very still; her whole strength went from her. And, seeing this, he put an arm about her and led her to a bench within the alley. He knew it well; it had been used by many a lover – himself included. But now he had no desire to play a lover's part. She was but a child and she honoured him with her love. To love her as she desired would be only too easy; there was a passion within her childish frame and she had a most bewitching charm. But it could do neither of them any good and it might bring them both much harm. He had planned this meeting to bring her some comfort; now, at the misery in the white upturned face, he blamed himself for seeking her.

He went down upon one knee. 'Sweetheart,' he said. It was a word he had often used in her childhood, and knew, too late, he should not have used it now. 'Never look so sad! You are to be a great princess in Christendom. You are the rose of England, the jewel of Flanders. All men honour and love you . . .'

'And shall I love all men?'

'It is our Christian duty.'

'And you? Do you love all women?'

'I have not been blameless in the past,' he said. 'I trust with God's help to make amends. A man must keep constant to his marriage vows . . . if he may. But one woman I wear always in my heart; to my sweet sister I will for ever be constant!' And he took her by the hand.

'Sir, I have one brother and need no more,' she said, very proud, and took away her hand.

He bowed and left her. She sat upright and still until he was out of the darkness and into the sunlight. Then a passion of weeping took her. She loved him and he did not know it; or perhaps, knowing, did not care.

The Imperial ambassadors had arrived. They had brought with them their own copy of the treaty, signed and sealed, in

49

return for the one bearing the King of England's signature. They brought also a casket of jewels sent by the little groom, but chosen by his aunt, the Archduchess Margaret. Mary did not offer to look at them.

Chapter Seven

In December the ambassadors came from the Netherlands to celebrate the wedding.

'I had rather they stayed at home!' Mary said.

At Dover they were welcomed by the Prior of St Augustine and Sir Edward Poynings on the King's behalf. And so in high procession to Canterbury where the crowds stood to cheer them. And, having rested from the fatigues of their journey, the bridal party went on to London, which could always be trusted to put on a fine show. There was music and there were tapestries and banners, as well as ribands and laurel wreaths, all set with bright berries and every pretty thing winter can afford. For all the world loves a wedding and who cares if the bride be unwilling and the groom a child of eight?

At Richmond on the seventeenth day of December 1508 Mary was wedded by proxy to the little Prince of Castile. The King had determined to show the splendour of England which he had found so poor and made so rich. Even Mary had to own that never before had she seen such magnificence. The Presence Chamber was hung in rich silk of green and white, striped and stitched with raised roses of gold. Nine court cupboards were set with plate of pure gold. In the chapel, where Mass was to be said, shone images of gold set with jewels. Between the great hall and the chapel a small chamber hung with cloth of gold had been set aside for the bride.

'In this very room your mother w   , as you wait now,' my lady Guildford said. 'The ·   ge was none of your mother's choosing either; nor was it easy – your father is not an easy man. Yet she made and shaped her marriage as one makes and shapes a beautiful thing. What she could do, you can do. Married you must be; therefore for your mother's sake show yourself her daughter this day. Listen! They are coming to fetch the bride.' And seeing the fear in the girl's pale face: 'For the love of Christ show yourself your mother's true child.'

It was being done. She was being married and she wished herself dead. For one mad moment she wanted to cry out, *No! No!* But she remembered my lady Guildford's words and for her mother's sake stood calm and still; she was even smiling a little when she took the proxy groom's right hand in her own to make her declaration:

'I, Mary, by you, John, Lord of Berghes, commissioner of the most high and puissant Prince Charles, by the Grace of God Prince of Spain, Archduke of Austria and Duke of Burgundy, hereto, in your person and by his special commission, take the Lord Charles to my husband and spouse, to consent to him as my husband and spouse. And to him, and to you for him, I promise that henceforward, while I shall live, I will have, hold and repute him as my husband and spouse; and for this I plight my troth to him; and to you, for him. . . .'

She heard her own voice say the words clear and faultless and slow. But it was as though another voice uttered them, and deep in her heart her own voice crying the while. *The thing is done. It is done and can never be undone.* Her heart still crying within her, she took the nuptial kiss upon her lips, and upon her finger the nuptial ring. And now the register was being signed; so many signatures that sprawled themselves upon several pages. Then, music playing and trumpets sounding, they proceeded from the Presence Chamber to the chapel to hear Mass. Thence to the great dining-room where the

King showed the treasure of his plate. At the high table the King, his son and the ambassadors dined off pure gold; at an equal table, set also with gold, sat the King's mother, the Countess of Richmond, the bride and the Princess Catherine. The rest of the guests, seated in due order, dined, even to the lowest in rank, off pure silver. There was no base metal seen. And the diversity and richness of the food accorded well with the splendour of the service, so that the strangers looked from one to another, marvelling.

The King, eye watchful lest aught should go awry, noted the weariness of the bride, though still she carried herself with grace and courtesy. The father overcoming the King, he sent her leave to depart.

In the quiet of her closet she sat still as an image and let her women disrobe her. They removed the headdress and since, though virgin still, she was yet a wedded wife, they bound up her hair for a symbol and placed thereon the crown of the Princesses of Castile. Now she was, indeed, Mary of Castile, though she held the title of little worth beside her true name – Mary of England. When she had eaten a morsel of bread and sipped some wine, for eat meat she could not, she was commanded to the tourney, and thither she went, the Princess Catherine again bearing her train. In the gallery overlooking the ground and set aside for the royal ladies she took her place; but though her eyes were upon the jousting, she saw nothing. When a knight broke a lance in her honour and her ladies clapped, then she too lifted her hands; but all the while she made her mind a blank lest even now she disgrace herself with tears.

She lay awake on this her marriage night in her lonely bed. If marry she must, it should have been to a proper man she could learn to love. But they had given her to a child; they had cut her off from all men.

Everywhere the country rejoiced at her marriage; the red glow upon her ceiling told her of bonfires burning still, of oxen turning upon the spit, of cakes cast up into the air for sheer abundance of them, of wines and ales flowing free.

For three days Richmond was a round of festivities. There were hunting and hawking parties, there was bull-baiting and bear-baiting, there were tournaments, there were banquets and balls, there were mummers to perform the time-honoured masques. Knights jousted in honour of the bride; and it added to her grief that Charles Brandon bore away prize after prize and that she must bend to crown him. She could not escape her sense of loss; indeed, the sight of him forever beneath her eye, so handsome, so skilled and so debonair, served to feed her love; and when she must touch his hand in the dance – then passion flared.

The ambassadors were still in England when Mary received a letter from the child who was now her husband. A formal letter, beautifully written but cold and stilted; she found no pleasure in it.

Charles, Prince of Castile, to The Princess Mary.
Ma bonne compagnonne . . .

'How do we translate that?' she asked Lady Guildford.

'It is more than *friend*; it implies a relationship, a knowledge one of the other, a sharing of pleasure or work.'

'Then it is no word to use between him and me. Between us there's been no sharing; no, nor simple friendship; nor, do I trust to God, there ever shall be!'

'You are unkind, Madam.'

'Am I indeed? There's nothing in this letter save the signature but what might be written to . . . to a brother-in-arms. It is no letter to a wife.'

'A wife he has never seen,' Lady Guildford reminded her. She proceeded to translate the rest of the letter.

. . . as warmly as I can I recommend myself to your good grace. I have charged the Lord of Berghes, together with the other ambassadors sent into your country, to tell you everything about me and my affairs. I beg you to let me know through them of your good health, for that is the news I most desire, as the blessed Son of God knows. I pray to Him that, by His good grace, He will give you, my good *compagnonne*, all that your heart desires.

'There it is again, the word that means nothing, *compagnonne*. I believe the letter was written for him!'

My lady looked at the fine free Italian hand, written by one to whom the pen is familiar. She nodded. 'Yes, the only words I judge to be the Prince's own are the subscription. "Your loving husband Charles." It is written in a child's careful hand.'

'I can imagine it; his head close to the page. Writing slow, writing with care.'

'You must give him credit for that!' my lady said.

'Why so I should if the child were not my husband! The rest is the work, I make a guess, of some secretary. Yes, see! It is not only composed and written by him, but countersigned also. P. Hanneton.'

'A child so young he cannot write his own letters; yet husband enough to prevent my marriage with any other man on earth!'

She spoke with passion to her father's chaplain. Wolsey looked up from his writing in the small, bare room, its only furnishings a crucifix, a statue of the Virgin with a small lamp burning beneath; a table with writing materials, a chair and a stool. Had she been less blinded by her troubles, she must have noted the richness, the beauty of each single article.

'Never fret, Madam,' the young priest told her. 'For all this marriage, the Prince of Castile will never be your husband. I swear it! No, Madam, there's no magic in it; only a clear look upon the present to understand the future.'

'Then who shall be my husband? You know so much; tell me that!'

'Madam, we must wait to see; we must wait upon events to show the pattern. But certainly I can swear to this! You shall marry, but not Castile.' The certainty in the man could not fail to make its impression.

Yet still she could not be content. 'Then, priest, if I am not to be Princess of Castile, what of these jewels?' She held out a great ornament with a ruby and pearls. 'Blood and tears,' she said.

'The blood will not be yours.'

'But the tears?'

'All women must weep some or other time. Madam, you will certainly weep a little; but not believe it, for long!' And now his tone was so final she dared press the young man no further. She prayed he might be right; she feared to be sent from home to the court of the so-dreaded Archduchess Margaret. She wanted to laugh, to play a little . . . if she might with Charles Brandon. Her nuptial ring she wore upon the first joint of her ring-finger, where all might see it; but in the privacy of her closet she threw it from her; nor would she ever wear it save in public.

The King of England was a careful man. Maybe he and the Emperor Maximilian had known each other too long; certainly each knew the other would keep his word only so long as it suited him. Maybe, too, he was impressed by Wolsey. The chaplain had warned him also, that for all the treaties, the ambassadors and the wedding-ceremony, the marriage would be broken. And, for all his youth, the chaplain had a knack of being right. The King had already paid out the sum of fifty thousand gold crowns, part of the dowry; but had wisely asked for something tangible as a pledge of faith. Maximilian had sent a valuable jewel: a cluster of large diamonds set about a diamond larger still, and all of them a fine colour and shape. So great the jewel, it was known throughout Christendom as *la riche fleur-de-lys*.

Now, with Wolsey's doubts added to his own, the King, more than ever distrustful, made an addition to his will.

Since, at my own great cost, the Lady Mary, my daughter, has been openly and solemnly espoused to the Prince of Castile, the marriage shall, in due time, be completed. But if by my death or otherwise, it be dissolved, then with the consent of my Council, or the overseers of my will, she shall be married to some noble prince out of the realm of England, she shall receive the £50,000 for her dower. . . .

That should put an end to any trick the Habsburgs might try! Neither Maximilian nor his daughter would be anxious to throw their money away.

It was drawing very near to Christmas and Henry would have the ambassadors stay for the festivities; the longer they stayed, the more certain he might feel of their good faith. This they declined with gracious thanks and took their departure with gifts more showy than valuable.

Chapter Eight

The New Year of 1509 came in with gifts and merrymaking. Yet the merrymaking lacked heart. The King was plainly unwell. Always a quiet man he scarce opened his lips these days; he easily tired. He had never recovered from his illness of last year; he was fifty-two and clearly an old man. He had gone to Richmond for a little quiet, and there he found eternal quiet. In April the King died.

Mary felt her father's loss, missing him in his accustomed place as the figurehead of the State. He had been wise and dignified and old; she could not yet imagine the young Henry in that place. The court went into mourning; Mary and Catherine wore black of the new King's providing. Black the gowns were, but very rich and, setting off the fair colouring of both girls, seemed more like adornment than mourning. Henry fastened the *riche fleur-de-lys* in his black bonnet where it shone and sparkled; he refused to return it to its true owner though the Emperor offered to redeem it from his own purse.

There's no woman, be she ever so young and pretty who is not the prettier for a fine gown. Henry, who had been casting soft glances at Catherine, was fired afresh. He could scarce wait for his marriage. Rome had declared the ban on kinship lifted. Reluctant, Warham, Archbishop of Canterbury, had consented. And now, at last, the Council was satisfied.

In May the dead King was buried with all possible pomp and reverence. And in the first week of the following month Fuensalida, the Spanish Ambassador, signed the marriage document for his King. On the eleventh of June, Henry and

Catherine were wed at Greenwich, Archbishop Warham
conducting the service. A quiet marriage with little in the way
of festivities, as was proper, since it was so short a time since
the old King had been buried.

On the twenty-first day of June 1509, a fortnight after his
wedding and a week before his eighteenth birthday, the young
King rode with his Queen to the Tower; there according to
custom to spend three days in the lighter business that precedes
a crowning. He and the Queen received visitors – gentlemen
from the remoter parts of the realm and foreign gentlemen
come with congratulations and gifts. London was full of
people come to see the sights. The City had surpassed itself
with fine tapestries and with ribands and garlands of white
and gold and no other colour; for this crowning which
followed hard upon the burial of the late King it seemed right
and proper.

On the day of the coronation the King and Queen, beneath
the cloth of Estate, walked to the Abbey in the midst of the
great procession. The Queen and her ladies again wore white,
but the King was clad in a gown of crimson velvet, furred with
ermine; his coat beneath was a raised gold set with rubies,
emeralds, diamonds and pearls, and about his neck a great
chain of rubies. At the Abbey door stood the Archbishop of
York with other bishops to cense the royal pair, and within
waited a great company.

The King and Queen went to their places on the high dais;
beside the Queen, but a step below, stood the Princess Mary
rejoicing in her heart that Catherine was come at last to her
rightful place. Rapt and uplifted, she followed the glorious
ceremony.

My lord Archbishop Warham showed the young King to
the people, leading him to face the assembly at all points
saying, 'Do you receive, obey and take this noble prince for
your King?' And, so shining his looks, they could not contain
their joy but consented and acclaimed him with so great and so

sustained a voice, it seemed the windows must shatter with the sound of it.

How had her brother's marriage affected her own? Mary thought long upon the matter, and thought with some hope.

She asked her question of Lady Guildford.

'The Queen's marriages to my two brothers: they have already doubled the knot of kinship, moreover the Prince of Castile is own nephew to the Queen. That adds to the kinship, making a threefold knot, maybe a fourfold knot if you count my kinship with the Queen. Surely a knot there's no untying?'

'The lord Pope can, if he chooses, being God's voice on earth, cut through a fivefold knot, or a sixfold knot.'

'Can I not myself break through the knot of marriage? The Prince is under age and so am I. The marriage has not been consummated, nor can it be for some four or five years.'

'You can do no such thing. Your word is given. You cannot shame your brother with a broken promise and jilt the Prince with no reason! What should they think of you in Christendom?'

'Shame my brother? Marriages have been broken before. He all but broke his own. Jilt the Prince? He is so small there's no insult to his manhood. But give myself, all unwilling! There's shame indeed!'

'The shame is in breaking your word. Oh, Madam, Mary, my darling child, you can do nothing in the matter: nothing! Never set your heart on it!'

But for all that, Mary could not put from her mind the words Wolsey had said: 'You shall never marry in Spain.' Fantastic words in the circumstances, yet Wolsey must be listened to with respect. The new King had been quick to recognize his gifts. Besides, he liked the man; a churchman who did not disdain the sweets of the flesh and who made the fulfilment of his master's desires the first of his ambitions. Henry chose the eager cleric as his own almoner – a rich plum. And Wolsey made the young man's kingship sweet;

he worked continually upon the business of State, leaving Henry free for his pleasures. The King as yet troubled himself little with royal duties. He was scarce eighteen, he was newly wed and in love with his wife. And he was free for the first time of his father's watchful eyes, of his father's firm hand – that tight-closed hand. Upon every occasion he consulted Wolsey; and always Wolsey arranged all to meet his every whim. And now began that sequence of appointments leading him to ever-higher honours. There was nothing to which, in time, the man might not reach – Archbishop, Chancellor, even the triple crown itself – so long as he pleased the King. And please him he did!

It was now the spring of 1510; nearly a year since the old King had died, and the young King, impatient to be out of mourning, had already ordered new clothes for himself, for his wife and for his sister. There were doublets and hose, gowns and kirtles, rich silks and worked brocades. There were cloths of gold and of silver, and tissues sewn with jewels. Merchants the world over knew that, unlike his father, the young King bought what pleased him and did not count the cost; they had not yet learned that he did not always pay so readily! The Emperor's great jewel, the *riche fleur-de-lys*, the King still wore in his bonnet. Mary was glad to see it there. Though Maximilian had sent condolences upon her father's death and congratulations upon her brother's accession, no word had been said of her marriage. Hopefully she put the child-groom from her mind.

The English court was a garden full of flowering blooms and singing birds; and the finest flower of them all, the sweetest singer to Mary's mind, was Charles Brandon; of him she heard much, saw much. One forgot that he was a husband and father, save when he rode into the country to visit his family; then the court was dull, the King himself languished.

It was Brandon's idea that the King should take part in the masques. In secret Henry was shocked but amused – he was the *King*: how could he take a mummer's part? Such a thing had never happened in all Christendom! But soon enough Henry was won; he could dance, he could sing, he could comport himself better than the best. Let Christendom see and judge the English King.

Mary was delighted to play her part in so new, so charming, so delightful a venture; and that Brandon had designed it all was an added joy. He had designed the costumes, supervised the dances and chosen the music; for this first masque there should be no words. It was to be a secret; first there should be a banquet, then the surprise.

To Mary the banquet seemed interminable; she was filled top-to-toe with the most joyful excitement. Soon she must stand up with Brandon and take him by the hand. During the rehearsals she had waited for these moments with a longing that grew in strength. That longing was in her now.

After the banquet, the hall having been cleared and freshened, the dancing began. The King opened the ball leading the Queen, but presently some dozen of the dancers slipped away. Then, to the surprise of all, there entered six foreign ladies with six foreign gentlemen; they were dressed in the fashion of the East in blue and crimson. All were veiled to the waist in black gossamer, through which they could see while themselves remaining unseen.

The dancers stopped dancing, looking bewildered, as well they might. They look towards the King's place; it was empty – he must be somewhere among the dancers – but in her place sat Madam the Queen, smiling. The veiled dancers moved towards her great chair, saluted her in Eastern fashion, hands clasped above bowed heads. Then, taking hands, they moved into the middle of the hall. From behind a curtain unseen music began to play, and the six Eastern couples danced, moving at the hips as Eastern dancers do, clapping in time to the unseen music, casting off to the unseen music, meeting again to take hands; then the gentlemen bowed in Eastern fashion, and the ladies kneeled, hands clasped. The whole thing was an absurd and charming medley of English and pseudo-Eastern dancing; but it was new and it was unexpected.

There was a whispering and a wondering; who might these dancers be? Foreign lords and ladies or merely mummers? Was it proper to applaud them? Then from her place the Queen clapped and the whole court joined in the applause. At this the dancers stood upright and flung back their veils. The King, the King himself led the dances, together with his sister. At that the applause doubled, trebled, and could not be stilled until the King held up his hand for silence.

Going to her place on Brandon's arm, uplifted with joy at the touch of him, Mary heard Wolsey speak to the French Ambassador in a low voice, but clear enough to reach her ears and those of Fuensalida, the Spanish Ambassador, who stood nearby. 'Madam the Princess of England is the most beautiful lady in christendom.' *The Princess of England* he had called her, not *the Princess of Castile*. The French Ambassador bowed and nodded and smiled; but Fuensalida's face was of stone. . . . That Wolsey had called her the Princess of England gave Mary more pleasure than the compliment. That he had meant both herself and Fuensalida to hear, gave her even greater pleasure. No man ever overheard Wolsey say what he did not wish others to hear. Was it . . . could it be the whisper of a reprieve?

Chapter Nine

Charles Brandon looked at himself in the mirror; he was well pleased with what he saw. He could see the whole of his handsome face and shoulders; if he used two mirrors he could see the back of his head – a well-shaped head beneath the springing red-gold curls. Like the King he was elegant of waist, handsome of leg. But, in his own opinion, he was cleverer than the King. Couldn't Henry see that in Wolsey he was making a rod for his own back? As for himself: give Charles Brandon a chance and he'd prove himself – captain in war on land or sea, or else in the more difficult art of representing the King in the courts of Europe. He was, he knew, a man born to please; but at present the only chance he had of pleasing was as pleasure-maker for the King, and few could match him at that! In the second year of his reign Henry had knighted his favourite. He had, it seemed, pleased Madam the Princess Mary, too. Had she been in his stars, he might have hoped for her; married he was, but the marriage bond had been seen to fray and snap before this, as he knew. . . . Charles Brandon twirled the folds of his velvet embossed cloak, admiring its set upon his elegant shoulders.

Henry and Catherine were as happy as any married couple, young or old, and now, to add to their happiness, the Queen was pregnant. Henry was forever talking of his good fortune in securing such a treasure. 'She is the topmost jewel of my crown!' he would say, and cared not that he had said it all before; nor was she ever tired of hearing it. 'Her virtues shine

forth clearer every day; her beauty blossoms and increases.'
'Were we still free to choose, we would choose her again above
all ladies!'

In the first week of December 1510, Catherine went into
seclusion to bear her child. She chose Richmond for the birth-
place and Mary as her chief companion. The week before
Christmas the King joined his wife for the festive season. For
Mary it would be the less festive for Brandon's absence. He
was at home with his family (his wife, it seemed, was ailing);
but he would be joining them soon.

On New Year's Day, 1511, the Queen was delivered of a
son. Messengers sped across the sea with the good tidings; all
over the country joybells were set ringing; wine flowed, beef
turned upon the spit, prayers and alms were freely given. The
child was christened with great ceremony in the private chapel
at Richmond; the silver font used at the baptism of Henry
himself had been brought from Canterbury for the occasion.
The chapel was hung with arras so that the child might not
take cold, and extra braziers burned. The Archbishop of
Canterbury and the Earl of Surrey were godfathers.

Never was court so joyful, and the day after the close of the
Christmas festivities the King rode to the shrine of Our Lady
of Walsingham to give thanks for his son; and thence to
Westminster where the Queen joined him for her churching.
There followed jousts and feasts and masques. Those jousts
Mary would always remember. All the champions stood ready
armed, their esquires in attendance, their heralds displaying
their masters' quarterings. All there save he for whom her
heart longed – Charles Brandon. Presently, the trumpets lifted
to sound the opening; there came in a poor man in a russet
gown that, kneeling before the Queen, asked that he might
tilt in her honour. Amazed she was, yet so kindly she could not
refuse, though her queenly honour was at stake. He stood
upright then, off went the russet gown – and there stood
Brandon, Brandon himself, his rich armour damascened in
gold. Unexpected as he was, Mary saw him at that moment,
in the shock of surprise, more beautiful than ever she had

remembered. He was back – back again where her eyes could see him, and though the King himself jousted at his best, it was Brandon who bore away the prizes.

Suddenly, the happy days were cut short. There was no longer cause for rejoicing. The Queen wore an anxious look, her eyes dark-ringed, blue-shadowed. Mary went with her to visit the royal babe, her nephew; she did not like what she saw. The babe looked frail, he lay languid. Above the Queen's head, bent over the cradle, Mary sent an inquiring look to the rocker; the woman answered with a barely perceptible shake of the head.

On the twenty-second of February the seven-week-old babe, child of England's hope, died.

The King appeared dazed by his misfortune, but he was a sanguine creature. He put aside his most bitter disappointment. 'We are young,' he told the stricken mother, as his father had done before him, 'and God stands where He was.' And soon, pretending an acceptance he did not feel, he acted himself into some sort of cheerfulness, redoubling his prayers, his kindness and his alms. Catherine, too, knew her duty; a Queen cannot remain ever shrouded in her grief. She took up her duties where she had laid them down, and performed them with all pleasantness; how much she wept in the privacy of her own closet not even Mary knew.

For Mary time seemed to stand still and she was glad it should be so; there was little to remind her of her marriage. One thing alone had changed; the Prince of Castile, now eleven years old, wrote his letters himself. They were as formal as ever; they showed no more warmth than those once written for him, nor anything but polite interest. Had it not been for the Archduchess Margaret it is likely that the marriage would have been broken by sheer inanition, but in this year of 1511 the Duke of Gueldres, egged on by France, attacked Burgundy – Burgundy that the Archduchess held for her nephew the Prince of Castile. Now indeed the marriage contract with the

Princess of England was remembered; the contract that promised mutual help against the enemy. Ferdinand, as Regent of Castile, owed a duty to his grandson in the matter, but did as little as possible, distrusting both the Emperor and England. Let those two allies do what they could in the affair! A gesture was called for and in July Henry sent fifteen hundred men. They captured a village or two, and to show her gratitude, and maybe as a reminder also, the Archduchess gave each returning soldier a suit of white and green, red and yellow, symbolizing the union between England and Castile.

Walking with heavy heart in the gardens of Westminster, Mary came upon Wolsey. He was dressed in fine lawn and rich silk, as became one who was now a Privy Councillor. And, for all he was the youngest of the Councillors, he promised soon to wield more power than any.

'Well, priest' she said, 'it seems that for all your promise I am still wed to this child my father chose for me.'

He sent her a small, subtle smile. No wonder, Mary thought, women ran mad for him. He had but to smile, so she had heard, to find his bed well warmed. He had not, as yet, grown fat with good living; he was slender, he was elegant. Builder's son he might be, but the university had done much for him and he himself much more. His voice was pleasing, his diction courtly, his bearing dignified yet gracious, his whole person fine in the extreme.

'Madam,' he said, and he did not, nor ever would address her as Princess of Castile. 'What I said I hold to! Once the lord your brother was hot for this marriage; now he is lukewarm. So it is with the Emperor also. You were to have been sent to the Netherlands within three months of your marriage; yet it was not demanded. It has till now suited neither side. The Emperor sees greater advantage from a different marriage – to his grandson's loss and our great gain. So far he has been content that the matter stand still; the Prince is over-young to make question of a bedding, but the break will come; and it will be easy. For, if no one else speak, then, Madam, you shall speak for yourself!'

He answered her clear amazement. 'When bride and groom are under age at the time of their marriage, such a marriage, if it be not consummated, may at the desire of one or the other . . . *their own desire*, be held null and void. No man need speak for you in the matter, Madam; it is enough that you speak yourself, alone!'

'I should never dare it; my brother would never forgive me!'

'There are circumstances when your brother might welcome it. Madam, the break will come. You have my promise. And I promise one thing more; within a shorter time than you could believe possible, England will be at one with France.'

'It cannot be so, Wolsey. There is now not a twofold but a threefold alliance – England, the Emperor and King Ferdinand of Spain, standing all together.'

'Madam, you may believe me. On the break with Spain and the alliance with France I pledge my ring.' He held out his thumb, a thick thumb that alone betrayed his birth, and on it a great sapphire.

'I cannot believe it. Yet I would fain wear your sapphire, my lord, so I gain courage.'

'Why, so you shall. And sooner than you think.' He took the ring from his thumb.

'It is somewhat large!' He smiled again. 'My goldsmith shall have it ready in good time!'

She was to wear his sapphire. But had she known what his prophecy entailed, she had liefer by far he had kept it on his own thick thumb.

Chapter Ten

The year 1512 came in; it was kept as usual with merrymaking. In March Mary was sixteen: another occasion for celebrating. For Margaret in distant Scotland it was a happy year also. In April she, who had seen her first three children die, gave birth to a son; a fine healthy boy that looked to live. To Mary, her sister was now a faraway figure, but she prayed that Margaret's present happiness in the child would continue; and indeed the child grew strong, a self-willed little boy to succeed his father – the young future James V. In contrast, Catherine, carrying now her second child, found her hope ended in sorrow. The baby, once more a little prince, died. Again the young parents showed courage, prayed, gave to the poor . . . but the King was not so sanguine as before.

That same year Brandon was left a widower, with two small daughters. Anne was not missed at court; she had lived for the most part of her short married life in the country and her death was scarce noticed. Brandon, though he carried himself in sober fashion, did not appear inconsolable; his black velvets, set off with jewels at throat and ear, showed to the more advantage the brightness of his cheeks, his hair and his eyes.

Mary's heart sprang upwards. It was useless to hope, as she knew well, but, for all that, hope was not to be denied. Anne was dead; and the wife of his annulled marriage – if marriage it might be called – had married again. Brandon was free, free! Half of her way was clear. And the other half? Wolsey had sworn she should never be wife to Charles of Castile; he had done more, he had shown her the way to break up the marriage.

'Brandon has lost two wives and looks to take another!' Lady Guildford let the information drop, as if it were casual news.

Mary lifted a white face from her stitching; pain struck as though the needle found her heart instead of the linen. The draining of her blood would have told its tale to one who knew her far less well than my lady.

'Yes' – and now Lady Guildford was gentle and careful – 'there is talk that he is to wed Eliza Grey, the little Lady Lisle. She's a viscountess in her own right and heir to the Lisle lands. A great match. Her birth is far above his and,' she struck firmly, 'it would make him a rich man. The King would give Brandon anything in the world or almost!' And now she struck again, her eyes full upon the girl. 'So he will create him my Lord Lisle that he may marry the heiress and she keep her father's title.'

'A cheap way of giving!' Mary said, seeming-careless, her heart sick with anger and jealousy.

'Not so! The King has wardship of the girl; he could sell her to the highest bidder . . . and the bidding would be high! A young child, a rich heiress, a fine family and a great title!'

'Then Brandon must wait for his treasure; she is what? Seven? Eight?'

'Nine,' my lady said firmly, 'and growing fast.'

'Nine!' Mary said scornful, remembering her young cold prince. 'Much water must flow under the bridge before he take her to his bed!'

'She's worth waiting for; and maybe he'll have worked his way through another wife or so before then . . . I should pity the child wed to a man some twenty years older than she, save I doubt she'll take him.'

'Eighteen years!' Mary amended very quick. 'And she'll not refuse him, nor any lady in Christendom!'

'Well, we must wait and see!' Lady Guildford said, very brisk for she pitied the girl's white looks. She had not realized the full measure of this girl's adoration; hero-worship, admiration for a handsome face she had thought it. But now, disaster

70

suddenly falling, my lady saw that Mary's heart was irrevocably set: Brandon was her true love and would be for ever.

The King's great new ship, the *Sovereign*, Charles Brandon in command, had been burnt at sea and every soul lost. Mary heard the news, eyes darkened; she put out a blind hand and fell to the ground. She lay on her bed unspeaking, eating nothing, and through the endless hours she prayed that one, at least, had been spared.

Later in the day my lady came with a cup of hot soup laced with wine. 'You may drink with a good heart!' she said. 'It was not the *Sovereign*, but the *Regent*!' Mary stared, not at first taking in the news; then she came stumbling from her bed to throw herself before her prie-dieu in a passion of thanks.

It was only afterwards, with shame, she remembered that, thanking God, she had not spared a thought for those who had gone, flaming like torches, into the bitter sea, nor of the women whose hearts were broken that day.

Unprovoked, the French had burnt the great ship and would burn every ship they could lay hands on; burn without mercy. So much for Wolsey's prophecy; looking into the future, he'd tripped over himself. It would be the Spanish match for her unless . . . unless she herself had courage to break it. When she thought of standing up, alone, facing the Council, facing her brother in his outraged majesty, her heart dropped dead, cold as stone. For her part Lady Guildford prayed that the Spanish match be hurried on before the girl's desperation led her to rashness.

Spain and the Netherlands were already skirmishing on French soil; by his sister's marriage-treaty Henry was bound to aid Spain. In the spring of 1513 he was called upon to honour the treaty; he did so the more willingly because of the burning of his great ship, the *Regent*. Besides, he had not as yet proved himself in battle. He was eager now to show all Christendom the valour of a truly Christian prince. Mustering his forces together in Calais, he did not doubt of his victories that should bring France to her knees. Thereafter, home again, he would arrange for his sister's shipment to the Netherlands, according to the treaty. He loved her and would miss her; but she showed herself overfond of her own way . . . overfond, too, it would seem, of Brandon.

For a month or more his captains and troops had been cruising; a noble fleet well found. So many ships, men said, were never seen upon the sea before. On the last day of that month the King himself was to sail, carrying with him the Bishops of Durham and Winchester, the Lord Privy Seal and the Viscount Lisle. Mary could not endure to think of him by the hated name that linked him with another, though the other was but a child.

The King was leaving the Queen as Regent, and this was no empty title. She would sit in his place at the head of the Council to govern the kingdom, to raise yet more forces . . . and the money to pay for them. To Mary, Catherine now seemed older than her years; once she had seemed younger. With the loss of her two children she had lost something of her spirits, something of her health. She was now not only a woman once more pregnant, she was Queen Regent.

The King and Brandon were for France. After this, thought Mary, God alone knew when she would see Brandon again. These days they never met save in public. See him alone she must – and there was one man, one man only, she dared trust to send a message – her friend and Brandon's. It was never easy to speak with Wolsey unless he chose to speak with you. She watched his comings and his goings; and, seeing him at last come from the King's closet, she placed herself in his path.

'Wolsey,' she said, 'will you please to help me?'

He knew full well what she wanted and was not minded to entangle himself in the affair.

'If I may with honour, Madam,' he said, and cast a significant look upon the papers he carried, reminding her of his many duties before the King sailed.

'I must see Brandon once – once only – to take a last farewell.'

'And a last farewell it could be, for this could be reckoned a treason in him; it could set a rope about his neck.' He turned away, but suddenly turned round again. 'Madam, there's a certain yew alley . . .' and he bent his strange opaque eyes upon her. 'The gentleman walks there sometimes . . . betwixt four and five in the morning is his favoured time.'

She stared at him amazed. His choice of the yew alley as the trysting place could be no accident. He had known of her meeting with Brandon there, all those years ago, and he chose to remind her now that nothing could ever be hidden from him. As for my lord's time of walking – he knew as well as she that Brandon was no early riser, but she could count on Wolsey ensuring that in the next day or two he would rise betimes.

In the thin light of dawn she crept cloaked over the dew-wet grass; within the yew alley it was black as night, a darkness comfortable to the hope in her heart, but silent as the grave. No one was there. Then, suddenly, he was with her, her love, dressed in black velvet that he might the less be seen.

She stood very still. There was anger in her, but there was high passion, too, which he knew could well set his own aflame. She was beautiful and she loved him. To take her in his arms was an urgent temptation: his arms about her, his lips on hers, and she would know a searing desire that would haunt her for ever, whereas he would be affected only for a little, and that but slightly. Her white face, upturned beseechingly in the darkness, moved him with pity. It was comfort he must give her now, comfort, nothing more.

He took her hand and lifted it to his lips. She had been unbearably stirred by the mere sight of him; now his kiss upon her hand was too much. It was not the salute of a courtier, but – and this she was too young to realize – it was not the tribute of a lover either. He put his arm about her lest she fall, and led her to a bench. Falling on his knee before her, he drew from his doublet a chain of gold, on which hung neither cross, nor miniature, nor any other jewel, but a ring – her ring.

'If I may not wear it for all to see, at least I wear none other.'
His hands, usually so richly bedecked, were bare. 'And, so long as this' – he held up the betrothal finger – 'remains uncircled you shall know you are my heart's delight. As for you, I ask no promise. You are a wedded wife . . .'

At that she cried out in pain: 'Wedded, but no wife, no wife!'

'But you shall be forever my heart's darling.'

And that, he thought, was true enough. A knight must have his lady; in her name he would fight, in any tournament bear her token. But . . . a man must marry, beget children to carry on his name and inheritance. So it must be with him! But before she was carried into the Netherlands, he would not look about him for another wife; that at least he would spare her.

And so simple was she, so young, so confused and over-thrown by this first love of hers, that though all he had said was 'You shall be forever my heart's darling', promising her no faithfulness, it was enough.

Yet not quite enough. Surely he must take her in his arms, surely she must have his kiss . . . one kiss. She said, because she was young and afraid before his greater experience, 'Wolsey swears my marriage shall never take place.'

'And I swear it will and must – indeed you are already wed – though Wolsey has a strange way of being right. But, my love, if not this marriage, why then another, as great or greater. But never a marriage with one of my blood – simple though gentle. So we take our farewell. . . .' And it was time indeed, for even through the darkness of the yew alley light was stealing. He stood up and lifted both her hands to his lips; she sprang to her feet, her arms went about him; she kissed him full upon the lips.

'Now . . . whatever may befall, you are sealed to me for ever!' she said.

The kiss was magic. He longed to seize the moment, to kiss her upon those inviting lips, to kiss her again and again . . . never to stop.

But magic goes as quickly as it comes. And this very day

he was for France. He did not return her kiss – it was a certain honesty in him. He walked backwards from her as though she were a queen, and so was gone.

Mary and Catherine had ridden with the King in a vast company to see him off in his ship; though Catherine, Mary thought, had done better to stay at home. But for all her quiet she could be obstinate, as she was to show later. Back from Greenwich the procession had ridden, lacking the King and his fighting peers; back to an austere court where there could be no feasting nor masquing; back to a court where hearts would be hollow with fear for news of husbands or sons killed in battle . . . or for lovers.

Chapter Eleven

On the twenty-first of July 1513, the King of England with his vast host, his cavalry, his foot soldiers, his bowmen, gunners and the twelve great guns called – half in jest and half in awe – 'The Apostles', marched for Thérouanne.

It was then that James IV of Scotland struck. He was England's sworn ally, yet he had already sent ships to help the French. He had sent his herald Lyon to the King of England commanding him to leave France forthwith on pain of a Scots invasion of England. 'The lord King of Scotland has suffered overmuch wrong from England. He is not minded to see his brother of France wrongfully attacked. Withdraw, sir, at once or expect the worst!'

For Scotland it was now or never. The King of England being absent and the best part of his armies across the sea, what better chance? Regarding neither his Christian oath nor yet the marriage-tie with England, the Scots King made preparations to carry war into that country.

His Queen, yet again expecting child, sought to dissuade him, kneeling before him with tears. She had been beset by fearful dreams of his death.

'Dreams! They are but women's fancies!'

'That may be. But it is no dream, sir, that you have but one living son, and he a little babe. It is no dream that you leave this land of yours to the government of one, a weak woman, whose inheritance must be bloody war. Do not think, sir, England is undefended; many men my brother has taken with him, but many remain for her defence!'

He paid no heed. His wife she was . . . but she was also the King of England's sister.

The Scots had crossed the Border; they had seized Norham Castle and all but razed it to the ground. They were laying waste the countryside with fire and sword.

Her brother, as Margaret had known, was no fool to leave his country undefended. Thomas, Earl of Surrey, had begged to accompany the army into France; Henry had refused, he wanted Surrey where he was – in command of the North.

Surrey marched through Yorkshire calling all men to arms; thence to Newcastle and, with no loss of time, reached Alnwick. There, according to his orders, he found awaiting him Lord Dacre, Lord Clifford, Lord Scrope and many another; tried soldiers all and each with his own men well armed behind him. He found also such common folk as would serve their King, many that themselves had escaped the cruelty of the Scots, but whose wives and children had not escaped. He marched with an army of thirty thousand at his back.

On the seventh of September Surrey caught sight of the enemy and his heart sank. He had not expected so huge a force, at sixty thousand men double the size of his own, nor so impregnable a position. James had massed his men upon a hill called Flodden Edge; a path climbed to the Edge, a path so narrow that two men or three at the most could climb it abreast. Behind Flodden Edge rose the Cheviots, outstretched as though for further protection. The Scottish army stood within a natural fortress.

To attack here would be suicide. The English commander turned about and the Scots, laughing at so instant a retreat, jeered and sent arrows whistling at his men's backs. Surrey, consulting with his captains, decided to go roundabout to take the enemy by surprise. His forces marched north-east, crossing the river Till, as though towards Scotland. From Flodden Edge the Scots watched, and speculated.

Then James moved his army from their fine position on Flodden Edge, the thing Surrey desired with all his heart. But first the Scots King ordered the camp to be burned – the Edge with its heather, the tents and all such objects as could be discarded – and the wind, blowing towards the English, prevented them from seeing what course the enemy took. Under cover of smoke the Scots moved towards Branxton Hill, a mile from Flodden; and there, as the air cleared of smoke, the two armies came face to face.

A messenger brought the news to Queen Catherine.

'We have brought Madam the Queen the Scottish King's bloody coat. On Flodden Field, the Scots King died, the flower of Scotland's nobility around him. There's not a noble family but mourns its dead today . . . and of common soldiers ten thousand Scots at least.'

Two men laid out the coat, stiff and brown with a man's heart's blood. Catherine and Mary looked at it in silence. *This was victory* . . . but Margaret their sister was a widow; her little eighteen-month-old son was fatherless and, unbelievably, himself now King of Scots.

Yet joy must be shown, praise given, and the great news sent to Henry in France.

Outside Thérouanne on the twelfth of August the allies had met, the Emperor offering himself – from courtesy, and Henry from courtesy refused his offer, though he had been sorely tempted – as a private in the English King's army. They crossed the river Lys and entirely surrounded the town.

'Madam,' said the messenger kneeling before Catherine at Westminster, 'the French, trying to get food through to Thérouanne, were routed at Guinegatte. They could not run away fast enough; so fast they were like horses spurred. We call it the "Battle of the Spurs". And, Madam, a great store of arms as well as provisions have been taken. And many noble prisoners, one a prize indeed! None other than the Duke of Longueville, own cousin to the French King, and worth a fortune.'

Thérouanne fell, and the allies stayed in the town to celebrate their victory; on the fifth of September they marched out, with trumpets and drums and flags flying, for Tournai.

Mary rejoiced in her brother's victory and in the certainty

of further victory at Tournai. But when she heard that Madam the Archduchess Margaret had invited the King and all his suite to her capital, Lille, in order to enliven for a little the dull sitting-down before Tournai, then a cold hand fell upon her heart. She feared the invitation greatly, for one did not hold feasts in the midst of a siege; it meant that the Archduchess was showing a most warm friendship. And what could this mean but the confirmation of her own match with Castile? Her unhappiness was increased by the fragments of gossip that came from Lille. Brandon was there; the Archduchess showed him special favour; he in his turn had declared her without equal in Christendom. Every word brought Mary a deeper sense of despair.

At Lille all was set for the entertainment of the English King; a pleasant break in the austerity of war. To England came news of feasting and dancing; of jousts and tournaments. Madame Margaret had planned her entertainment less for the King than for the man on whom her fancy had lighted. She had arranged a special tournament for the two champions that were to answer all comers – the King and Brandon. A tent hung with cloth of gold had been assigned to them, with twenty-four knights in purple and gold in attendance. The champions were dressed alike in fine steel armour damascened in gold; and so alike in their looks that they might have been brothers. The esquires, bearing their arms, stood by their horses that were trapped in velvet and hung with chains of pure gold. Before the actual jousting, the two champions rode about the lists to the plaudits of the great throng; then they came to do reverence to the ladies.

In England the Queen and Mary heard every detail. How the Archduchess and Brandon had looked long into each other's eyes; how, with Brandon kneeling, Madam Margaret had taken her scarf embroidered with pearls and tied it about his arm, proclaiming him her own especial knight; how the jousting had begun and the Lord Lisle had borne away prize after prize.

And so, all ending with feasting and dancing, back again to

the grim business of war, back to Tournai. 'My lucky city', Henry called it; and the men, themselves smelling good luck, needed no urging in the fight. The twelve 'Apostles' thundered; within a few days the walls were breached; Brandon, first to enter, captured a tower and with his men held it. On the twenty-first of September the city capitulated. At the head of his troops, Henry rode in to receive the keys and to take the city's homage. It was indeed Henry's lucky city, a city that carried on a great trade in tapestries, in linen and in cloth with the chief markets of France and the Netherlands.

'My lord King will arrive home early next month,' a messenger said. 'He stays in Tournai to celebrate the victory, to renew his alliance with Spain and the Netherlands, and to make final arrangements for the departure of Madam the Princess of Castile.'

Mary stood stone-still; only her eyes moved, flickering sideways to Wolsey. He returned her glance with that subtle, secret smile.

This time it brought her no reassurance.

The allies were celebrating. Henry had besought the Archduchess Margaret to visit him in 'my good city of Tournai' that he might make fitting return for her honourable entertainment at Lille, and she had brought with her her nephew, the thirteen-year-old Prince of Castile. A very great banquet was held, the tables set all with silver plate, save the King's table whereon every piece was of gold. And with all court ceremony there were served over one hundred dishes: soups of eight kinds, thick and clear; of fish, ten sorts in curious sauces; meats of every kind dressed in divers fashions; some in white sauces lozenged in gold or with raised crusts as it might be a castle or a beast; there were birds, from peacocks adorned with their own feathers to larks in green jelly. There were puddings and pies, there were custards and blancmanges; there were subtleties of many devices including a model of Tournai itself in coloured sugars.

To the King of England, but halfway through the banquet, arrived his Queen's letter with news of the victory at Flodden; and with the letter a piece of the Scots King's blood-stained coat, in which he had died.

Henry stood up to announce the victory and to tilt the square of blood-stained coat for all to see; then he called for rose-water to wash away the contamination. Catherine's letter he laid aside and went on to sample the next dish. It was later, in the privacy of his closet, that he read the letter and was moved by her love and pride in him. For one brief moment he thought of Margaret, his sister, widowed now with one young child and carrying another. He brushed the thought aside. Her sorrows were none of his making; the blame lay upon that rash husband of hers. If she needed advice he would give it – though she was not one for taking advice. Did she need help he would give it – so it were not too costly. . . .

Of Mary, his younger sister, he thought long and carefully. Was this the moment to close the deal with the Emperor and send the girl to Lille? The consummation of the marriage could not much longer be deferred; the boy was already thirteen. Or should he hold his hand – see what France, her allies the Scots soundly beaten, the towns of Thérouanne and Tournai taken, had to offer? It was a question.

There was constant coming and going between Tournai and Lille. Tales were winging across the Channel, spiteful birds to peck at Mary's heart.

Wolsey came seeking her in her closet, a letter in his hand.

'I have heard from Ambassador Wingfield; undoubtedly there has been love-play of a sort between the Archduchess Margaret and Brandon. But more, Madam; Wingfield sends me a copy of a letter he has received from the lady herself. That she has lost her head over Brandon there can be no doubt; but her father's clear-expressed anger and her own wits bid her deny any part in such tales. She protests her innocence overmuch. She writes:

. . . . You may well know, my Lord Ambassador, the great love and trust that the King bears to the personage there is no need to name; also the virtue and grace of that personage. You must consider also the desire he showed to do me service. When I considered all these things I felt bound to show unto him all honour and pleasure, which seemed agreeable to the King, his good master, who spoke to me to ask if the good will I bear to that same gentleman might stretch to marriage. . . .

'But' – and Mary's pallor was not lost on the observant eye watching her – 'surely the King and he and she, all three, know it could never come to pass – the marriage of a simple gentleman to one of the royal blood. The Emperor would forbid it!'

'The King might do something in the matter to make it more acceptable,' Wolsey suggested suavely, but went on to reassure her. 'Let the King do what he will, however, it would all be useless. The Emperor will have none of it. She writes to say she has refused. She has told the King that to show Brandon such favour was out of the question. And so, according to herself, she put Brandon off; but day by day King Henry was at her until she confessed that it would cause her much grief to lose the gentleman's company.'

Yes, Mary could understand that.

'But' – and again Wolsey cast his eye upon the letter – 'when the day of departing drew near, the gentleman sought her in private to press her harder than ever: "You are too young to remain thus a widow! In my country ladies remarry at fifty years and at three-score also." But she said, "I never had the will to do so; I was too unfortunate in my husbands."

'And the King, your brother, took her hand and placed it within that of Brandon, and made her promise – the two handlocked – that howsoever she should be pressed by her father, she should not make an alliance with any prince in the world until Brandon return again. Then the King made Brandon swear that same vow; and swear he did never to marry nor to take any mistress without her command, but remain her life-long, right humble servant.'

And now Mary was so pale Wolsey feared she must fall; he

led her to a chair and brought her a little wine. When she showed more of colour in her cheeks, he said, very kind, 'You need have no concern. She'll not change her mind. She has had, as she says, too much bad luck in marriage to risk it a third time. But now,' he added, smiling, 'the Archduchess says gossip is so loud and so wide that she must not show her goodwill towards Brandon as before.'

. . . I dare not write to him even though it be on the King's business; nor dare I even speak of him. I am constrained to treat him in all ways like a stranger, at least before folk . . . .

And now she leaves her own troubles – if troubles they be – and speaks of you, Madam.'

Mary's hand flew to her heart. Only too easy to guess what was coming.

'She says she looks forward to the coming of Madam the Princess of Castile into Calais that you may be truly wed to the Prince in his own person.'

'By my sweet Jesus, so do not I! Were I free as she is, I'd marry the man of my choice. Pity me, Wolsey, that I must soon wed in his own person the wretched Charles of Castile . . .

'He may well be called wretched that is promised to the fairest princess of Christendom that he shall never have!'

'This is no time for nonsense, Wolsey! How much longer do you play your game with me?'

'It is no game, Madam. You'll never wed Castile; upon that I wager my head!'

'Then you look to be a headless man!' she said and departed comfortless.

Chapter Twelve

The fighting was over; but still the King must remain abroad to sign a new treaty. And very pleasant it was with constant festivities and England, Spain and the Netherlands joined in brotherhood against the common enemy, France. 'Let France look to herself,' so each man swore.

Much of the negotiations dealt with the marriage of the Prince of Castile and the Princess Mary of England. The royal families were to meet in Calais the July following, to solemnize and to consummate the marriage: no loophole left! The Prince would then be fourteen and the Princess eighteen. The Archduchess had cajoled a promise from Henry that, in default of heirs of his own body, he would settle the crowns of England and Ireland upon Mary and her heirs. It was a promise, a promise in words only, to sweeten affairs. But the word, written or spoken, made little difference to Henry. He would do as he chose when he chose, and, besides, his wife was again with child: why should he hesitate? In any case, he had no mind to do anything for James' son or, since Margaret was pregnant, any other child she might have by the traitor of Flodden.

On the fifteenth of October the treaty was finally concluded; and after much embracing and swearing of eternal brotherhood, the King sailed for home.

Mary was cast-down and desolate. All summer in spite of her own forebodings she had had some little hope. The King was away and Wolsey confident that she should never wed Castile.

She was drooping like a flower when she met Wolsey walking proud as a king in the gardens at Westminster.

'Well, Wolsey!' she challenged him. 'What of your promise now? My wedding day is fixed to the very day, the fifteenth of July of the coming year. How may I trust you, when all the while the preparations are going forward, and my trousseau a-making? And she – that woman that plays my Lord Lisle as a fish – is to have the last word in my gowns. My brother has writ it plain to her and has sent me a copy that I may hold myself obedient to her "greater wisdom" in such matters. It is the final insult. See for yourself, priest!' And she pulled the letter from her pocket.

> ... Forasmuch as the King's pleasure is that my lady the Princess's apparel shall be according to the fashion and manner of these parts, the King's grace has provided all cloth of every sort for her; and he prays that you will devise the making thereof in such a manner as shall best please you. ...

'It is like my brother to think of fashion and propriety – and not at all of me in this marriage. Let me tell you,' and she sobbed, 'it is one more lash across my heart that the woman I heartily detest should not only have devised my marriage but the very clothes I must wear!'

'Madam, such words were rash indeed, unless spoken to me, to me alone. Me you can trust! I am your friend. And so I say once more – you shall wed neither the husband of her choosing nor wear the gowns of her devising.'

And though all had been sealed, double and triple-sealed, he still wore his air of certain knowledge.

The King and Brandon were home again, borne triumphant upon the wings of success, but not for all her watching for his comings and goings, not for all her planning, could Mary catch Brandon alone. The King kept him forever by him; in the hunt, in the masque, in the practice of arms and in the Council-chamber those two were forever together.

She had taken to walking alone in the yew alley; it suited her changing moods, its close leafage keeping out the autumn sunlight suited her more sombre moments; and, in happier mood, how could she forget that here he had knelt and called her his heart's darling? And here by chance she found him – or was it chance? He was sitting pensive upon the bench – that bench before which he had knelt holding out the ring, her ring, warm from his heart. Her feet made no noise upon the ground; she had time enough to consider how she would greet him.

He raised his head as she drew nearer, and at the sight of her his face went warm with pleasure . . . or was it shame? Shame that he had not sought her out?

He rose and swept off his bonnet, and she, though her heart was beating in her throat, said, calm enough, 'It is the first time, my lord, I have had the pleasure of seeing you alone since you were in France. How does your lordship?'

'My lordship fares the better for seeing Madam the Princess.'

'I should suppose the charms of Lille outweigh those of London.'

'There's no place holds charm for me save when I may see the Princess Mary.'

'I should not have thought it.'

'You may believe it – even if I see her but at a distance.'

'Distance would seem the proper measure. And soon the distance will be greater. Within a little time I am to be sent to my husband.' And for all her brave words her voice faltered in her throat.

'Then I must feast my eyes while I may. After that I care not whether I be alive or dead.'

'Oh, my lord, all Christendom knows you for a very gallant gentleman, and especially a certain Archduchess!' And then, in spite of herself, 'Is she *so* beautiful?'

He nodded. 'She is at her beauty's peak.'

'There are some men like their fruit overripe.' Stung, she was a little spiteful; he liked her the better for it.

'It is a coarse taste,' he told her. 'For myself I like my fruit green, where it may ripen.'

'Green fruit ripens but with the heat; lacking that heat it must fall and rot.'

'You need not fear that last. A man shall warm you in his bed.'

'No man but a child; a dull, cold child. My fruit, alas, must fall and rot.'

'Never think it. It is no child but a youth, and shall make a most proper man. Dull he is not, nor cold neither. Beautiful you are, Madam, and clever with it; but you, even you, shall have your work cut out to keep him faithful.'

'I shall not try.'

'Him – him alone? Or any may you might wed?'

'Him. Him alone!' she cried out passionate. 'And he is the man I am to wed. But let me tell you this, my lord. If I loved the man I married, before I'd let him stray, I'd die – and he also!'

At such passion he raised his brows; it lent him a questioning, smiling look that maddened her. 'I think you know nothing of love!' she cried out. 'You wedded two wives, if wedded is the word. The first you abandoned for a better match; and when you had done well enough with the second, back you went to number one. And she dying soon after, it did not grieve you overmuch. Now you are to take a third wife – so they say. Shall it be the full-blown Archduchess or the little green bud of a girl, Eliza Grey? Her title you have taken already, my Lord Lisle. Why not the little girl with it? Well, which of the two shall it be?'

'Neither, as God hears me!'

'There's much to gain either side,' and she was mocking still. 'You have but to weigh and choose. Your heart is well disciplined; you may love where you will.'

'That you do not nor cannot believe – especially in this place!' He sent her a long, steady look.

'The Archduchess is perhaps the better bargain; and nearer to your age!' And, though she mocked still, the wings of her heart were lifting.

'I should never have her. A man should never wed above himself in rank.'

'Should he not? What of Anne Browne, or the Lady Mortimer, or the little Viscountess Lisle?'

He swept the words aside, impatient. 'The Archduchess,' he said, 'is not for any man. She is overmasterful; she cherishes her power. She uses it as a whip on a man's bare back. Oh, not with me! She can play the sweet very well. She is over-clever for a simple man! I know her well.'

'Being no simple man, but one able and willing to match her in her games! What of the reported exchange of rings between you?'

'A trifle, a mere jesting. Her heart was never engaged, nor mine, neither.'

'That is scarce gallant.'

'A man must speak the truth when he speaks to his heart's love.'

'Lucky if she may believe you, your heart's love – if such a one truly exists.'

'She exists – thanks to God – even if she be not for me. She is, alas, not in my stars.' And he bowed himself low before her.

And now that his meaning was plain she could do nothing but stand, eyes fixed upon him, unmoving, unspeaking.

He unbuttoned his doublet at the neck; and there upon a fine chain – her ring.

'My lord,' and she thrust down the joy in her heart, 'you are right and I am not in your stars. Shall I not take it back?'

'Not unless your heart is changed.' He waited, and since she said nothing to that, slipped it back into its place. He drew the signet from his thumb. 'Take this instead!'

'Shall you play the same game you played at Tournai . . . or was it Lille?' And she must give no sign of the heart melting within her . . . and like to be broken.

'This is no game. You gave me your ring of your own free will; and with love – as I think. If your heart be changed – why then, you shall have it again. If not, take my ring and my heart with it.'

She shook her head at that; she was fearful not for herself alone but for him; for him also.

He took her hand and turned it palm upwards. He put his ring within her palm, dropped a kiss to lie beside it, and closed her hand tight upon kiss and ring. 'So we keep something of each other!' he said.

'You are crazy-mad!' she cried out, and now she was frightened indeed. For him to wear her ring as a knight might wear a lady's hidden favour was one thing; this looked over-much like a secret betrothal. 'There can be nothing between us two, ever. I am *wed*.'

'If you can call it *wed*. Nor does your husband seem in haste to claim you. As for me, I shall never wed if it be not with you. I swear it.' And he turned himself about and was gone.

For all her visits to Our Lady of Walsingham, for all the King's prayers and her own, Catherine lost this last child she had been expecting. She had been wed some four years and there was as yet no living child. Mourning her loss, Catherine could yet accept it from the hand of God; in His own time He would send them a son. But Henry had already felt his first sickening doubt. Could it be that they had offended God? Did He not approve of their marriage? Catherine had sworn she was a virgin, and that long before there was any question of marriage between them; she had sworn it when it had been to her advantage to say she might be carrying the future King of England. Taking her on his bridal night, he had been too eager about the business; she had cried out sharply once or twice, and he had taken it as a sign of her virginity – but she had lain in his brother's bed. Had his brother taken her maidenhood, she herself unknowing? Could it have been done while she slept? It was over-late for doubting now. He had done better to give the matter more thought before their marriage, had the midwives examine her . . . but he had been in love. And she? He had never known her to lie; and in this matter, especially, would she, for their souls' sake, have dared to lie?

But still . . . but still . . . If his brother had taken her maidenhood, whether she had known it or not, then this marriage was incestuous. And there was no way of knowing . . . none. He loved her still; but not with his first eager passion. She was a pretty creature, gentle and kind, loving himself only next to God; and she was no fool either – those wits of hers were sharp. A pretty woman she still was, but in a way that now appealed less to him. She was thinner and she was no longer gay. He liked his women pleasantly plump; and he liked them gay.

That Henry had his doubts of her virginity at their marriage never entered Catherine's head. She had spoken the truth and he had believed her. Her faith in Henry was as absolute as her faith in God. But Mary read him more truly; when she prayed for her own deliverance from the Spanish match, she prayed for Catherine's happiness also.

Chapter Thirteen

In spite of compliments and gifts, in spite of the actual wedding-day fixed, the sweetness between England and the Netherlands seemed to have gone sour. The Archduchess was as eager as ever; the fault lay with the Emperor who made now this excuse and now that – and not one of them worth a fig.

Henry began to fume; his pride was touched. But Mary began to hope once more, and Brandon, though he dared not hope, took full advantage of the respite. She was too loving, too sweet, not to enjoy while he might. They met continually in the yew arbour to clasp and to kiss; it was all the love they were likely to enjoy. At the first moment of the meeting Brandon would slip her ring from his doublet, put it first to her mouth and then to his, and then put it back. It was a ritual.

In late October when leaves lay slippery upon the sodden ground and the mist shrouding up from the river gave little need for lover's caution, Brandon came to the trysting-place, kicking moodily at the leaves that clung sticky to his boots.

'Now you are more than ever out of my stars,' he said. 'Not that you were ever in them!' He took three backward paces and made the deep bow one makes to royalty; but now she knew it for mockery.

Mary's heart went sick. He had not brought forth the ring nor offered to kiss as much as her hand; his whole manner put a distance between them – and she all afire for the touch of him.

'What I tell you is a secret not to be spoken of as yet and concerns a promise made by your brother to Madam the Archduchess. The King himself told me. It puts beyond any man's doubting that the Spanish marriage shall take place!'

And she standing silent and afraid, he went on, 'Madam, I think I stand in the presence of the future Queen of England.'

'You are always one for a jest,' she said and let out her breath in pure relief. 'But at this one I cannot laugh; it is not a jest to my liking.'

'It is no jest. I said "I think"; almost I might have said, "I am sure." The King has promised Madam Margaret – by word of mouth only: even he would not dare set it down in writing – that should he have no heirs of his own body, the crown, Parliament willing – and when has he not done with Parliament as he would? – shall pass to you and to the heirs of your body.'

'This is plain nonsense!' Mary answered. 'It may have been *said*, to bring my laggard husband to the mating-point, but it cannot happen. The Queen is young enough to bear children yet . . .'

'She has lost three babes already. The King fears she cannot bear a child that will live.'

'It is not so; and God forbid it should be so! My lord, I implore you, never breathe such a thing! Let one whisper of this arrangement reach her and it will break her heart.'

'From me there shall be no word. The promise is secret as the grave. None knows of it but the King, the Archduchess and myself. Not even Wolsey; and he is set against the match and would break it if he could!'

'It is a promise that can never be kept. But even were it true – the cruel thing you say of the Queen . . .'

'Not I but God says it.'

'God has not spoken His last word; we must be content to bide His time. But were it true, there's my sister Margaret: her claim comes first.'

'The King would not for anything in this world she should have the crown. While he was fighting in France who but her husband stabbed him in the back? James paid for that treason with his own death but the wound of that stabbing remains. Nor has she herself shown she is a Queen to keep her country in peace; Scotland is loud with noise of quarrelling. And have you forgot? There's their own private quarrel. There is much anger between them.'

Mary had not forgotten. Their brother Arthur had bequeathed to Margaret his own personal treasure of jewels and gold plate. They were to have gone first to his father for life – which they had done – and then to Margaret. But young Henry had shown that same passion for property, that same determination to keep every piece of his sister's legacy as he had done in keeping the *riche fleur-de-lys*. Margaret, keeping down her hot spirit, had written more than once and very lovingly that her property be sent to her. Henry had taken no heed, and this rankling had played its part in the Scots' attack that had ended in Flodden.

'The jewels my brother may keep – if he will. They are his possessions and who may stay him? But the crown is another matter. It must go to its rightful owner; and that owner, my lord, is neither my sister nor myself. It is the child that shall be born of the King's marriage. We should do better to pray for the Queen than to dispose of the crown of England.'

'What a little spitfire it is!' And he was laughing. 'Well, since you are not to have the crown, and since you are not bedded with Castile, you are still my sweetheart.' And he kissed her, and she him, which was more to her taste than empty talk of a crown.

The year of 1514 came in. That it should prove a year to alter the whole pattern of their lives neither Mary nor Brandon then guessed; but to Wolsey it was no surprise. He had planned their course, and upon that course hung his own; and his indomitable will brought it about.

Catherine was pregnant again, for the fourth time; she believed that by God's mercy she would give England its heir in November. The King was cheerful at the prospect and for the time being put away his doubts. There was very much on his mind. There was still much coming and going between the King and the Archduchess concerning the Spanish marriage;

93

letters and messages had been carried backwards and forwards between England and the Netherlands – carried chiefly by the hand of Brandon. Henry himself, royal pride more than ever stung, chafed at the insolence of the delay.

Quite suddenly, in February with no intimation whatsoever, the King created Brandon Duke of Suffolk. There were but two dukedoms in the whole of England – Norfolk and Buckingham. And not only that, but the dukedom of Suffolk was semi-royal: it had belonged to the dispossessed de la Poles, Plantagenets of pure royal blood.

So sudden, so unprecedented an honour! To raise at one stroke a commoner – his title Lisle an empty courtesy merely! Not the English court alone but the courts of Christendom, astonished, were asking why?

Mary's heart was a singing bird. To her there could be but one answer: to raise Brandon to her own level. How should her heart not sing? Wolsey knew why, and his answer was quite different.

'Sir' – he had been forever at the King – 'the Spanish marriage would seem to hang fire. If it is ever to be consummated,' and Wolsey intended that it never should be; he had better plans for his King and for England, 'we need a friend at the Netherlands court. Brandon and the Archduchess have more than a liking each for the other. A marriage between his daughter and a mere commoner – for Lisle's title must go back whence it came if he does not marry the little Grey – the Emperor would never countenance it. Raise Brandon, make him a duke – Suffolk's title has fallen empty. So you make him worthy of the lady. I think then the Emperor can make no real objection, and the lady herself be more than willing. Those two shall wed and you shall have forever a friend in the Netherlands court.'

'Brandon needs no gilding. In himself he's fit for any lady in Christendom.'

'True, sir; but a little gilding hurts no man, and an English duke is an English duke!'

To get Brandon out of the way was no bad idea; Henry,

though he loved the man, knew of the fondness between Mary and his friend; of the depth of her passion he did not know.

So now Brandon was a duke! But though he was received with even greater respect and some affection in the court of the Archduchess, there was still no formal talk of Mary being sent to Lille, or of any consummation of the marriage. Although, like her brother's, her pride was stung, she was well pleased to wait. As long as she remained a virgin nothing was irrevocable.

The year moved on, and now it was June. Catherine carried herself serenely yet with care; Margaret, who had given birth in April to the posthumous son of James IV, later wed the young Earl of Angus, unpopular and dissolute. Gossip was hot with her name. She had added to the number of her enemies, and taken from the number of her friends.

Brandon, in all his new glories, was disporting himself as ambassador to the Netherlands. To Mary, without him, the time seemed long, and the court dull; her heart forever fearful and jealous. And still Brandon remained at Lille, and still the Emperor hung back. It was no fault of Madam the Archduchess. She had written to her father again and again to warn him that the King of England would not much longer endure this putting-off of his sister's marriage. She reminded him of the heavy fine he must pay if, through him, Henry declared the marriage void. She reminded him that it had been made for the good of the Low Countries – peace, trade and the crushing of France – and that, the marriage failing, all those good things they must forfeit.

Henry, one ear attentive to Wolsey and no longer eager for the marriage, was yet determined that the blame for the broken pact should not fall upon himself. He too wrote to the Emperor, declaring that every last thing promised on his side in the contract had been fulfilled. What now? He had his answer both from the Council of Flanders and from the Emperor himself.

It was ill-convenient to receive Madam the Princess at the time arranged, the Council declared, giving one reason and another – and not one sufficient. The Emperor's excuses, too, were poor enough. He refused Calais for the wedding, saying he feared the plague. There was no more plague in Calais than in any other place, and this being pointed out, he declared Calais too small for so great an occasion. He suggested Malines or Antwerp.

The King of England was touched to the quick in his pride; he was even more inclined to listen to Wolsey's whispering. 'The Emperor is playing a double game. He has another match in view for his grandson. He and the boy's other grandfather are secretly negotiating peace with France; the peace to be crowned by marriage between the Prince of Castile and the French King's daughter, the Princess Renée. But the Emperor is devious in his ways. He has no intention of losing one royal bride until he is truly handfast with the other. And more, much more, sir. The boy's other grandfather swears openly that if the English match should take place he'll disinherit his grandson. Charles will forfeit his title of Prince of Castile, and he shall never be its king; nor will he ever inherit Aragon or any of the other Spanish possessions either in Europe or in the New World. And of course,' Wolsey went on thoughtful, 'there will be no royal dower, either!'

'I do not believe it; nor can I believe it. Even from Spain who would believe in such treachery?'

'Call it policy, sir, and it becomes understandable. But, whatever you choose to call it, fact is fact and truth is truth!'

Henry's blue eyes reddened, seemed to sink into his head so they looked half their size. The small mouth, compressed, was all but lost in the golden beard. He turned, as ever, to Wolsey. 'What now, my friend, what now?'

'You may leave it to me, sir,' Wolsey promised.

Henry went about angry, sulky, thoughtful; Mary was jubilant but dared not show it. 'Surely, surely,' she told my lady Guildford, 'Brandon must be recalled.'

'What then?' my lady asked, cold and cautious.

'If my lord of Suffolk be considered good enough for an

Emperor's daughter, can it be denied that he is good enough for me, that am but daughter to a King?'

Wolsey sought out Mary where she walked in the gardens of Westminster, unable to hide her joy, so light her heart, so dancing her step.

'Well, Madam Princess. I keep my ring, I think. You shall give me another equal in value to the one I would have given you. I said you would not wed in Spain, nor shall you ever; for very pride the lord King would not allow it. And now I make another prophecy, Madam; mark it well! Before the end of this very year – and it is now June – you shall be wed. You shall make a better marriage than with Castile; and therewith you, the King and the whole country shall be content.' And for all Mary's pressing he would say no more.

He had set Mary wondering. Who could the man be, this magnificent groom that was better than Castile? Not Francis of Valois, heir to the old and sickly King of France? He was but late-married to the King's daughter Claude. A German princeling? That would not be a better marriage. No! the marriage to please herself, the King and the people – surely it must be Brandon, Brandon who had now a semi-royal dukedom. Yes, that must be it. She was to wed Brandon, an Englishman, a duke, the King's friend and her heart's love; of whom de Brezille had written, 'He is a second King'.

The Emperor, fearing lest both royal brides slip from his hand – for who could trust France? – and not aware that the King of England had knowledge of his plans, sent his ambassadors to assure Henry of his good intentions in the matter; the delay was temporary only!

Henry received them with courtesy, giving no hint that he knew of the Emperor's perfidy. He fêted them, he devised amusements, he invited them aboard his new ship just finished. Let them carry home news of his new fleet abuilding, some ships of which were ready to put to sea. Let that act as a warning to any that would turn enemy. The new ship shone magnificent, gleaming, formidable. Aboard her, ready with gracious greetings, stood the Queen, already showing promise of her child; next to her Mary, beautiful and bewitching. Let them report to the Emperor of the prize he was losing. And, indeed, reporting as they had been bidden, they could find no words good enough to describe the charms of the young English princess . . . 'the loveliest girl in Christendom', they called her; and were careful to leave a copy of their report where it might be found. They need not have troubled. Wolsey took care that no ambassador's letter left, but it was seen and copied.

It pleased Mary – a pardonable vanity – to copy it for herself.

. . . I think I never saw anyone so beautiful; she is extremely graceful and has the most charming manners possible. I think had you but seen her, you would never rest until she was with you. I assure you she is well educated. . . .

They were convinced, or so they said, that she was in love with the Prince of Castile.

. . . She loves Monsieur exceedingly and it seems to me that the best way to please her is to talk about him . . .

Well, so much was true! Now that she knew her brother no longer favoured the match, she took a perverse pleasure hearing them waste their breath in praise of their prince.

Chapter Fourteen

'Madam, it is time for you to act!' So said Wolsey when he paid an urgent call on Mary in her manor of Wanstead, a house rather than a palace to which she was glad to escape for a while from the turmoil of the court. 'The Emperor's ambassadors flatter the lord King; and he, though he has spoken outright about the continued delay, now appears to be somewhat softened by their flatteries. Now, Madam, to me it is clear that the Emperor means to marry his grandson elsewhere . . .'

'Pray God he does!'

'You'll not lose your prayers. But how the matter is done is of importance. It will not add to the King's glory either here or in the rest of Christendom that his sister has been . . . rejected.' He spoke that last word with a delicate emphasis and had the satisfaction of seeing the girl's cheeks redden furiously. 'It is time now for the Princess herself to act.'

'And yet Wolsey, how may I set myself against the King?'

'You will be working for the King, *with* the King. It is hard for him, under their flatteries, to break the marriage; you will save him much embarrassment. He is not one to enjoy a slap in the face; nor, Madam, I fancy, are you! You yourself must administer the slapping to the Emperor and to Spain. *You* must refuse the match, and do it at once!'

'*How* can I do it? What must I do?'

'Madam, the matter is simple.' He spoke quietly for a matter of minutes. At the end she looked at him aghast. He smiled and repeated, 'Simple it is; but it will take courage.'

July 1514 was drawing to its end when Mary summoned her friends in the King's Council, together with those other lords that disliked the Spanish match and had said so very plainly. There came to her my lord Duke of Norfolk, the new Duke of Suffolk back from the Netherlands, my lords the Bishops of Winchester and of Durham, the Earl of Worcester and Wolsey himself, now my lord Bishop of Lincoln and looking soon – if his plan succeeded – to be much more, very much more.

To these, her great chamberlain at her side, Mary spoke; and though her heart shook within her, her voice was firm – it was a royal Tudor who was speaking.

'My lords. I have summoned you to hear my resolve; a resolve to which I am come after much thought and many prayers. It is a resolve from which I shall never depart. Never in this world shall I fulfil the contract made for me with the Prince of Castile. The match is not possible. It is the constant endeavour of those nearest the Prince to fill him with dislike and distrust of me, his bride, and of my lord the King that was his brother-in-arms. To the contract I gave my word; so much is true, but my heart never. Yet, though I was but a young child then, that word I should have kept. But now it seems to me that the contract is already broken, in secret, by the lord Emperor himself. Am I to wait for all Christendom to hear of his rejection of me? No, my lords. I have the right, as I believe, to break it and to break it openly. I am no shuttlecock, my lords, to be tossed this way and that between the Netherlands and Spain. I am a princess of the royal house of Tudor, granddaughter, daughter and sister of a king. I have come to my decision, not through any threat or persuasion, but of myself, alone. This paper that lies before me is of my own devising and my own will. Now, here in your presence, I shall sign it.'

She waited; but never a man spoke, not even Wolsey that had engineered the whole affair. Nor had they come unprepared; Wolsey had seen to that. Yet the thing itself actually taking place beneath their eyes was so much more than they expected. They were not sure, either, that it did not smack of treason.

'My lords' – she heard her voice of authority tremble; she was, after all, only eighteen and she was defying the King who did not take kindly to defiance; and defying him in the face of all Christendom – 'I have summoned you here as my friends; not only to strengthen myself with your goodwill in this matter but to entreat that you intercede with the lord King. Beg him, as you be true men, not to show me his displeasure; for in all things, even in this, I am and shall be conformable to his pleasure. . . . But, my lords, I am shamed, shamed to the very heart, at being thus batted about, as it were in sport! There is no woman, be she queen or beggar, can nor should endure it.'

And in the silence, still unbroken, she took up the quill and signed herself in her rightful name, Mary, Princess of England – never more would she call herself Princess of Castile.

They looked from one to the other, waiting each that another might speak. Each man was concerned for his part in the matter. Useless to say they had played no part; by their very presence they were involved . . . yet, short of laying hands upon her, no man could have stopped her.

In the silence Wolsey stepped forward.

'Madam Princess, we have had no hand in this affair, as you yourself will testify.' Well, she was prepared for that. It was his way of protecting them all – herself not least. To have summoned these lords, and they attending and knowing the reason, might be accounted an act of treason in them all – a treason for which she was responsible – and so much the worse for her. As an act of outraged and justified pride by her, and her alone, it might well pass with little more than the King's expressed anger and maybe a short banishment from court. She had had, after all, good cause for complaint and the King himself was no longer wholehearted for the match.

And, she nodding, Wolsey continued, 'Indeed I make bold to say that, had we known the object of this meeting, not a single man of us had dared attend. Yet this I say – and I speak for myself alone – in this my mind is the mind of Madam the Princess. Before God I will do my best.'

She heard assent, half-fearful, from the others.

'My lords, I do thank you with all my heart. This kindness I shall remember and treasure for ever – '

They bowed and departed, Wolsey leading them; and from him never a sign that he had known aught, much less advised her in the matter.

She had won . . . for the moment. She wondered, if the King changed his mind to favour the Spanish match, whether she should find courage for continued rebellion. Head between her hands, she considered what might be the outcome. If the King should need to save his face she might yet find herself in the Tower. In spite of the kindness between them, he would spare her little more than any other who offended. Since he had assumed the crown he had changed; or, rather, faults in character – if one dared call them so – had deepened. Always he had been self-willed; now, given a King's authority, there was no way of moving him save by subtlety, flattery and coaxing. Always he had prized his possessions, yet he had known the difference between *meum* and *tuum*. Now he cast his eyes upon the possessions of others and took what he wanted – Margaret's legacy, the Emperor's rich jewel.

Now she had acted on her own authority, casting her brother's policies to the four winds. She need not have been troubled. She was not to know that what she had done today was by the King's nod – and no word spoken.

She was still at her thinking when Wolsey sent to ask permission to wait upon her.

'Madam,' said that most subtle of men, 'what you did today was both clever . . . and dangerous.'

'Not cleverness, my lord, but sickness of the heart; and what is danger beside such sickness?'

'I had thought, Madam, you acted from a most proper pride. I trust it was not from the green sickness young people mistake for love.'

'It was both, my lord . . . and I think you knew it.'

'I did not know it! That you have a liking for a certain gentleman I know well enough; but to suppose you could let it weigh a hairsbreadth in such an affair. . . !' He blew out his lips in contempt. 'If such be the case, then, Madam, I am not so sure as to your cleverness; but very sure as to your danger. Madam Princess, the green sickness could be a fatal sickness – if you allow it. Not you yourself alone but another could suffer for it.'

She did not pretend not to understand.

'Will you help me, my lord?' And she was very humble.

'The cure is in your own hands. It lies, Madam, in a humble obedience to the King in all things. Oh, not in the Spanish marriage; that is over and done with! But some displeasure he must show.'

'My lord, I will take whatever punishment he sees fit to lay upon me.'

'It will be light enough; no more than a few hot words. His heart is now set against the Spanish marriage. But' – and he was preparing his way with some care – 'you cannot afford to flout the lord King a second time; not in anything, in anything at all.'

'I am at one with you there, my lord; I had not dared this first time save that desperation and your good advice together drove me.'

'You may not find my advice so agreeable in the future, though be sure it will always be for your good; nor may you find yourself at one with me.'

'Meaning, my lord?'

He spread his thick white hand on which his sapphire still shone. 'Who knows? One thing only I do know; I cannot, even for you, Madam, stand a second time against my King!'

'I would not ask it; nor should there be need. Ah well,' and she laughed a little, 'the Castile marriage is broken, and the King forgives me – what more can I ask?' And she turned upon her toes. 'Why trouble ourselves as to the future?'

'Why indeed?' He knew very well why. When she gave

him her heartfelt thanks, his face did not change; and did not change when she knelt for his blessing.

My lord the new Duke of Suffolk paced his chamber in Whitehall. The old manor house left to him by his uncle was being enlarged and made worthy of a duke; he would call it Suffolk Court. From his window he could see it rising upon the south bank. When it was finished it would be fine as any palace; worthy of the King himself, with its gardens stretching down to the river, its gardens sheltering it from the highway; its maze, its lakes, its flowerbeds and lawns, its walls upon which peaches should ripen. And he would furnish it fit for a King . . . fit for a princess . . . *a princess.*

He came from his admiration of his new house to consider the new turn of events.

'She herself declared the marriage broken. I did not know her intention, did not even guess at it. In this Wanstead business I am safe; not the King even can blame me. . . .' He thanked her in his heart for her discretion. 'Had she asked me in this matter what should I have said? *Obey the King!* I must have told her, though it broke my heart.'

But it would not have broken his heart, and he knew it. She was beautiful, she was gifted; she was lovable and loving . . . 'But *love*, that's another matter! What is love? One loves; one stops loving; one loves again. It is man's nature. All things equal, I could be happy with so delightful a creature. But for how long? Even with her I'd not swear to be forever faithful. But things are not equal. The King has no mind I should take his sister; he has, indeed, more than a mind that I should marry the Archduchess. . . .'

He paused to consider that lady.

'A curious creature, both formidable and silly. In the strength of her will and knowledge of her power – formidable; in her love-play – silly! Yet I played those little games; why not? She's handsome enough. So I pleased the King, the lady, and for a short time – myself. But marry with her – had I the

104

chance – I could not. What should I be then but the Regent's husband? Her lap-dog to be taken notice of – when she had time. I could have helped no one; not the King, still less myself. God be thanked, I had no chance. The Emperor made his displeasure clear, and for that I am forever in his debt. I am an Englishman. I like English ways. I am an English duke to marry where I please – save for the King's sister. She alone is barred. What then? I am freer than any prince that must marry where he's bid . . .

'Yet to tell myself the truth, if I might choose, I'd take the Princess. . . .'

Again he took himself over the long catalogue of the advantages. That she was the King's sister was not – even should the King approve – one of them. He was an ambitious man, but – the King's brother-in-law! That might cut two ways: the King, for all his easy-seeming friendship, was formidable and demanding. A wise man would not choose to come into too close a relationship with him. Besides, Wolsey had spoken; had warned him off. He'd said little – but that little sufficient. Well, he was in no haste to wed. There were women aplenty for his bed; and meanwhile there was this delightful affair with the Princess Mary, an affair both innocent and passionate: a rare combination. He'd take his time; wait and see how things turned out.

He went to the window once more to look upon the pleasing sight of his growing palace.

Mary stayed at Wanstead alone save for Lady Guildford and Sir Ralph Verney, her chamberlain. She waited in fear for her brother's summons. Wolsey had said that the King would, in his secret heart, be pleased . . . but suppose Wolsey were wrong? He was human; he could make his mistakes. So she tormented herself.

The summons, when it came at last, left her no wiser. The King requested his dearest sister to wait on him at Westminster. The word 'dearest' meant nothing: it was the common formal usage. Save that he command her to the Tower, he would always use that word . . . and to the Tower he might yet command her.

For all it was high summer the countryside wore a sombre look; the trees had darkened their green; a storm threatened so that the sullen sun lent them a funereal appearance. And it was quiet too; quiet as the grave; save for the muted plop-plop of their horses in the dust, no sound. She noted with a sinking of the heart that no birds sang. Well, but in August one did not expect birds to sing! Yet for all that, her heart was still down; nor did it rise when the countryfolk came running from their houses with their posies and their cakes and their blessings. She longed for her journey to end, to know her fate. Had Brandon, she wondered, moved in the matter? She prayed he had sat quiet and done nothing. He did not, save perhaps by implication, come into the affair. She had acted for herself alone. Even had there been no Brandon she could not have endured the insult of continued delay. A wise man would say no word, give no hint even, he would wait . . . but lovers are seldom wise. *Was* he a lover? Yes, surely yes! They had met, they had kissed, they had exchanged vows . . . and he wore her ring within his breast.

They came into London by way of the Straight Ford through Bowe village and Stepney, and so to the White Chapel, where she bade the cavalcade halt, and into the church she went to pray for help. And so into London itself by way of Aldgate and through Fleet Street and out again to Westminster. There was no courage left in her; yet were it to be done again, she would do it.

As she rode into the Palace yard the storm broke; it was not, she thought, a good sign. The King had ordered her to her own apartments, and once there, he kept her waiting. And that was not a good sign, either. She sat alone but for Lady Guildford and could not hide her trembling. And all the time she told herself, 'I am a Tudor. I am not to be humbled and set aside'; so that when Wolsey, at long last, made his appearance, she greeted him with a quiet face.

'You have shown a proud spirit, Madam; now show a humble one!' And still he played a part as though he had no foreknowledge of what had passed at Wanstead; and certainly as though he had not counselled her therein. 'The lord King was not best pleased at the first, as you may imagine. Now the fancy takes him to declare himself amused. That so young a lady should take it upon herself to flout Spain and the Emperor is something of a novelty, if not a jest. Yet, Madam, you know him, how he can change from mirth to anger in the taking of a breath. Madam, have a care what you say and how you carry yourself, then all shall go well!'

'And . . . Brandon?' She could not forbear the unwise question.

He affected puzzlement. 'What has he to do in this affair? You are best, Madam, to leave my lord of Suffolk out of the reckoning. And now, Madam, the King will receive you.'

Chapter Fifteen

The King sat in his great chair, the *riche fleur-de-lys* in his bonnet; it was his sign of defiance to the Emperor.

Mary made her curtseys lower than etiquette demanded, at the door and in the middle of the room; the third brought her to his very feet. His head was turned in conversation; he went on talking and did not so much as look at her; he let her kneel. She knew very well it was his way when displeased but she had never suffered it herself. He did not acknowledge her by so much as a nod; he had indeed, it appeared, forgotten her. That was his way too; she must go on kneeling. She felt her knees trembling beneath the strain but still she must kneel.

Suddenly Henry looked up, the smile broadening upon his face.

'Why, sister,' he cried out, 'my most intrepid sister! And have you brought a herald, or do you come yourself to announce rebellion?'

'I come, sir, because you sent for me!' And she bowed her head to the very ground.

'Why, so I did! Oh sister, sister, I forgive you. You have made Spain and the Emperor sing small. It is a good jest and I love to laugh! As for Spain and the Emperor, we have no more need of them!' He bent forward and pinched her, none too lightly, upon the cheek. 'So stay you here and make us merry with the sight of you; but' – he lifted a finger asparkle with rings – 'never defy us again. We might not find the jest so merry!'

She was forgiven, yet not wholly, as she knew; the kneeling, the sharp pinch, together with those last words had been a warning. He would not warn her again! But she was free and Brandon was free. The shadow of a hated marriage had been lifted. She was young enough to enjoy her freedom; old enough to pray it should not last too long; that soon she might be wedded and bedded.

She was to have her wish; but not in the way she desired.

'It was as we thought.' Henry's smile broadened in a face already threatening fatness. 'An offer for my sister's hand; and no less a person than the King of France!'

'Sir, to unite with France against Spain and the Netherlands, there is great wisdom in your policy.'

Henry's hand went to his beard; he was preening himself more than a little. He had forgotten the notion was Wolsey's; and Wolsey knew better than to remind him now. The King was in high good humour; but with him one could never be sure.

'It is not a matter of policy alone. It is a matter, it seems, of *love*!' And he laughed aloud, the cruel laugh of the young that know little of the miseries of old age. 'Love! the poxy, swollen, disease-ridden old carcass! I doubt he'll survive his wedding night.'

Put into plain words the effect was horrifying. Even Wolsey, that had worked for the alliance and meant to benefit thereby, was shocked. Still, the alliance was the only right one; it would keep the balance of power even for years – if it did not tilt it slightly in favour of England. To be shocked by a few plain words was womanish.

'With such a bride, one night even should be sufficient . . .' and he returned the King's broad smile.

'I doubt. Still, love's a great revivifier so they say.' And the King laughed again. 'His cousin of Valois would have made a fitter mate for my sister; he's handsome, he's accomplished and the right age too, but two years older than she . . . and, above all, he's heir to the crown. Wolsey, why didn't we jump sooner? Why didn't we catch Valois before he married?'

'Our hands were tied, sir. The Princess was already married to Castile – or so we thought. But, sir, all works for the best. King Louis is free and our Princess is free. As you say, sir, love's a great rejuvenator, and our Princess is enough to make Methuselah himself lusty enough to beget an heir!'

And neither of them thought it necessary to consider what Mary herself might think. What she thought was no matter; she would do as she was told.

'The charm has already begun to work!' Henry told Wolsey a few days later. 'The old man's in a fever to wed.'

'Little wonder! The Duke of Longueville is own cousin to King Louis. He's been our prisoner since "the Spurs". You, sir, with your usual kindness gave him the freedom of the court. He's a gentleman with a French wit; he and Madam your sister have had many conversations together. He admires her as much as she deserves. He is forever writing home about her; his letters I have seen, naturally; it is my business. His opinion of her is golden, as it should be. He admires her above any woman in Christendom. She is, he writes, highly educated and speaks French and Latin well. She is elegant, she is sweet of nature. She carries herself like a queen, yet like a happy girl she can laugh and jest; yes, and take her part in the court masques you yourself have made so fashionable. For her singing and dancing he can find no word fit to sing their praises. And above all her beauty. She is not only the pearl of England, she's the pearl of Christendom. Is that not enough, sir, to make any mouth water?'

Henry nodded, well-pleased. The offer was balm to his smarting pride. But more, much more. The match must considerably strengthen England. By breaking the triple alliance against France, of which Henry himself was a sworn member – untrusted and untrusting – it would force France to keep faith with England. It must weaken the Emperor and the King of Spain; it would make a dint in the Austro-Spanish power – especially if Louis intended to give his daughter Renée to the Prince of Castile.

And Wolsey nodded, knowing his King's thoughts. 'And,'

he added, 'though it may not be mentioned in the same breath as high policies, King Louis has promised you shall have the sum the French King promised to Edward IV if he would lay down his claim to the French crown. It is a very great sum . . . some million gold crowns . . . It comes to one hundred thousand crowns a year!'

Henry's small eyes glistened; he licked his lips.

'Oh, we shall get more out of France; much more,' Wolsey promised this apt pupil. 'Old Louis would take anything at all in petticoats that would give him a son – were he capable of getting one. But Madam your sister! Young, fresh and beautiful – a gift from heaven!'

'But she!' For the first time Henry allowed himself some thought of her.

'Coax her, flatter her, bribe her; press hard upon England's need for this marriage. Never threaten. She has a fancy for Brandon, as we both know. But Brandon! Constancy's not in him. Well, that's a man's way; I've no quarrel with that! But she – a young girl's fancy; what is that to the glory of being Queen of France? Most girls would give their souls for that, never mind their bodies.'

'About this sister of mine I am not sure. She's fed full of romantic tales. *You* must bring her to it; *you*, Wolsey! You're her friend, her trusted friend; there's no one but you can do it. She confides in you; and you, in turn, have been good enough to confide in me. If you bring her round to this, then, Wolsey, when you succeed I'll not forget it!'

It was a mission – and a promise – after Wolsey's own heart. He was sorry for the girl, so young, so lusty, wedded to a half-corpse; but no doubt, having done her duty by her ancient husband she could, were she discreet, please herself. But let him, Wolsey, succeed in this and there was nothing he might not hope for. The see of York was empty. After York, Canterbury. After Canterbury? Cardinal of England, Papal Legate. And then . . . and then? Greater than all the princes of Christendom, he that all kings and emperors must obey: the Pope himself.

Mary was shocked into a sickness of silence when Wolsey first opened the most hateful matter of the French marriage; hateful as unexpected. She had been flattered by the praises of the Duke of Longueville; she had not been displeased that those same praises had been relayed to the King of France. The old man himself meant nothing to her. How could he? He was fifty-two and she eighteen. He was old enough to be her grandfather. Old . . . old . . . *old*.

'What is King Louis like?' she had asked the Duke and cared little enough what answer she might receive.

'He is good, he is gentle, he is generous to all; but especially to those he loves. They call him *Père du peuple.*'

What is King Louis like? She had asked this one and that. She gathered that he was old beyond his years . . . 'falling to pieces,' one young man said. Not only that, but he had never been young: he'd been *born* old. Even when he had come to the throne at thirty-five he'd been an old, tired man. Her picture of him began to grow. He was weak, his health continually bad. He was narrow-shouldered; he had been thin as a skeleton. Now he was grown swollen with the dropsy or some other sickness, and his head had grown enormous. He was simple and slow; in the way of a sick child, lovable. . . .

But now came Wolsey with his monstrous, his terrible, his unspeakable suggestion; yet for all that trying to make her believe that marriage with this pitiful, decayed creature was natural and good.

She sat there unable to speak, unable to put the horror into words; only her hand went up to her throat as though to keep down the vomit. Always in her heart she had known that her desire to marry none but Brandon was a dream, never to be fulfilled! Princes, she knew very well, were not their own masters. Wed she must; but the man should be clean, healthy, lusty.

'I'll not have him!' she said, when she had choked the sickness down. 'I'd rather take Castile.'

'Madam, you have no choice. You have rejected Castile, and had you not done so he had rejected you. But Madam, more than that; that you should marry the French King – it is not alone the lord King that commands it; it is the lord Pope, the Holy Father himself!'

And what, she wondered, had the Pope to do with her marriage?

'He sees no peace for Christendom but in this match. Beneath the Austro-Spanish alliance his own throne trembles.'

'Must I bolster the Pope with my own body?'

'If he asks it, but, Madam, leave him out of it for the moment. This country of ours that you so much love shall be secure in peace; and in all Christendom there shall be no King as great as Henry of England.'

His words did not touch her; she let them pass over her head.

'And yourself, Madam, you shall be a great queen and a happy one. King Louis has proved himself a kindly husband.'

'Good? How good?' she asked, very sharp. 'His first wife was daughter to his own King. Oh yes, he made sure of his value there! And she was good enough until he himself came to the throne. And then – divorce. Do you call that a good husband?'

'He did not marry his first wife of his own will. He was but fourteen. She was plain and lame, and her virtue was frightening.'

'Do you, my lord Bishop, find virtue frightening?'

'I speak, Madam, as a boy would think,' and he was in no way abashed. 'What could he do? Fourteen, fourteen only. Heir-presumptive, and all the weight of his King's authority upon him. Royal princes have no choice.'

'But they can keep their honour! And his second wife brought him Brittany in her pocket. There was a sweetener I make no doubt.'

'Madam, it was, I swear it, a happy marriage.'

'He has but very lately lost this second wife; and here he is agog to marry a third time. It seems he cannot wait.'

'No, Madam, he cannot. He's old, and has no son.'

'And I'm to provide that son?'

'With God's good help.'

'By God, I should need it. An immaculate conception – no less!'

'Madam, you come near to blasphemy.'

'Do I? Do I, indeed? All these years, twice wed and no son. Impotent – they say.'

'Not so. He has daughters . . . but by French law a woman may not inherit!'

'He has his heir, his cousin of Valois,' she said, indifferent.

'A man desires heirs of his own body.'

'Then let them alter their laws!'

'Madam' – and now he was altering his tack – 'you blame him for haste in marriage; but such haste betokens past happiness for him. And when he marries such a one as you, then that happiness shall be exceeded. . . .'

'The happiness of the French King is not my concern.'

'Madam, you may find it is! And your own happiness is certainly your concern. You shall have happiness beyond telling. The second wife had her will in every way; a free hand in everything. How much more you upon whom his heart is set?'

'Some women enjoy to wield the whip, others to feel it. But I am neither one nor the other. I like my own way, I do confess it. But not in all things. I'll wed no man but *is* a man . . .'

Again full horror of the situation swept over her. She said, hand at her throat where once more the vomit rose, 'You ask me to . . . to *do the act* with a diseased old man!'

That was indeed something of a pity, he thought, but dared not tell her so. He said instead, 'There's an old saying: *In the night all cats are grey.* A man's a man! Give him a son, and you may do as you choose – so you be secret in the matter.'

'*You* tell me that! *You*, a priest!'

'I am a practical man.' He was unmoved. 'I see no way for you but this marriage. I would have you make the best of it.'

'No!' she cried out passionate. 'Your advice may be sound for a Christian priest to give, but for a Christian woman to take . . . No! A thousand times *no*! I cannot nor I will take this King. I would die rather; you may believe it.'

'Take him you must! You talk of your duty as a Christian woman: to such a one her duty is plain – to obey the King and the Pope who speaks with the voice of God.'

Watching her stubbornness, he tried yet another argument. 'Remember your humiliation at the hands of Castile and the Emperor. The Princess of England cast off as though she were a serving-maid. Turn the tables; humiliate *them*. . . .' And, seeing her unmoved at this attempt to sting her pride, Wolsey played his trump card.

'Remember . . . one other. His danger.'

He saw her eyes darken with fear; and that fear no longer for herself. He pressed home his advantage.

'Madam, you spoke of dying. It is not *you* that shall die.'

He saw that she knew perfectly what he meant. She was in the net.

'No need, Madam, for me to spell it out. The King may love Brandon as a brother; but he'll spare no man that crosses his path; no, nor woman either. There is no hope for Brandon but in your consent. And, Madam, hark you well! Brandon himself consents to it. He did, indeed, advise the King in this matter.'

It might have been a dead woman sitting there stiff and still and white as ash; a woman struck dead with her fear.

'He was my love and you my friend . . . or so I thought,' she said at last, and there was neither bitterness nor anger in her voice. If the dead could speak it would be so, stiff-lipped, slow and cold.

'Madam. I speak not for him but for myself. I am your friend. And to prove it there's a thing to whisper in your ear. The King of France is very old and very sick. A gust of wind – and out he goes. Or with no gust, no gust at all. He cannot last long. Make his last days happy; thereafter be happy yourself.'

'My lord, you talk a great nonsense. How shall I be happy waiting for my husband to die? And how shall I be happy – a widow in France?'

He noted the word. 'Shall' she had said, not 'should' but 'shall'.

'How shall you be happy? You have, Madam, the wit to discover that for yourself.'

Chapter Sixteen

How shall I be happy – a widow in France? She had asked her question and received her answer. *A gust of wind – or no wind at all – and out he goes!* Wolsey had said it; Wolsey himself. And even Lady Guildford had said, 'You are now in a position to bargain.'

Think ahead; plan to put her love into a dead man's shoes and that man living still? It was not in her nature; to her, impulsive and not at all calculating, the thought was abominable. But her terrifying position, the hints that were less hints than advice, and less advice than threats, had done their work. She saw her way. She trembled still, but she was determined. She was rehearsing the words with which to bargain with the man who had been her kind brother, and was no wher dreaded King, when the summons came.

When she saw him seated beneath the canopy of Estate, his Queen beside him, and the full court in ordered rank either side, she knew the occasion for what it was; and for what it was not. He had ordered it thus to give her his commands, and no chance to speak.

'Sister,' he said, she kneeling before him, 'you and ourselves and all England are honoured this day. The most noble alliance is offered us; no less than marriage with King Louis of France himself.'

She said nothing; she went on kneeling. Her whole being, drawn in repulsion, could not permit her to say 'Yes'; the certain knowledge of her destiny and the promise she must ask of him dare not permit her to say 'No!' And since she still knelt there dumb and, a certain constraint arising from those that watched, the King, smiling and gay, raised her up, saying, 'Modesty in the face of so high a destiny is right and proper.' He led her to a stool at his feet, and there she sat, the smile carven upon her face as though in stone.

When the King had left for his closet, she made her way through the smiling, congratulating court, and sent to crave a private audience. And, this being granted, she knelt weeping, her careful speech all forgotten.

'Brother,' she said, and she could scarce speak for the tightness of her throat, 'am I dear to you?'

'Dear you have always been, but now dearer than our own soul. This day you have joined England and France in loving brotherhood; you have humiliated Spain that sought to humiliate us. And, sister, you bring not only peace but prosperity. Why,' and he could not contain his jubilation, 'France owes us a great deal of money – nigh on a million crowns. It will be paid to us – with interest, mark you – at the rate of one hundred thousand golden crowns per year. And that is but a beginning . . .'

'Shall you sell me for gold, brother?'

'Not for *gold*!' He tutted his impatience. 'But for peace; for power. Shall you despise these because gold comes with them – gold that is our just due? As for you, sister, I have seen no dislike of gold in you, ever. Your own dower, let me tell you, will be immense. You shall be the richest Queen in Christendom.'

'I want neither gold nor glory if I must take the old man with it!' The words were out of her mouth before she knew it. She trembled there upon her knees.

'Do you prefer quiet and time to think upon the matter?' and she knew he threatened the Tower. His eyes had gone very small, their light blue reddened by the suffusion of his blood. She knew the signs of his anger.

'Brother,' she said, 'you speak much of glory and honour; and it is indeed a great alliance . . . but what shall they sing of me in the streets – a young maid wed to an old diseased man?'

'What they sing they shall answer for.' And now the full mouth that, in spite of the reddening of the eyes, had been smiling still, pouted into a small button lost in the spreading gold of his beard. 'Sister, let us make an end of talking. You shall marry the French King whether you will or no. You have no choice.'

'Brother' – and it was now or never to press home the thing both Wolsey and Lady Guildford had hinted at – 'I will obey you. I shall marry the French King. I shall be to him all a wife should be. I'll scant no duty . . .' and she sickened at the words.

The redness of his eyes a little paled.

'But . . . should he die . . .'

'What then?'

'Then, should I wed a second time, let it, I beseech you, be a husband of my own choosing.'

'I make no *bargains*!' He sat pondering, chin in hand, eyes red, button mouth tight. Her heart sank lower yet; this, her one hope, was lost. Suddenly he let out a great laugh. 'So be it. Should the King your husband die, I'll not force you to a marriage. My hand upon it!'

She caught at his hand and kissed it. 'God shall bless you, as I do!'

And it never occurred to her that there was a catch in the bargain. He had promised only not to wed her against her will. He had not promised the thing she asked – a husband of her own choosing.

Henry was overjoyed. He had won advantages beyond his wildest dreams. Not only was his sister to make the greatest match in Christendom, thereby slapping Spain and the Netherlands full in the face; but he meant to keep that part of the dowry already paid as earnest of the Castilian marriage – a very great sum – together with the diamond *fleur-de-lys* that he would wear for ever in his bonnet: symbol of victory. And there were more spoils to come. Wild as any young man for his desired bride, the old groom had agreed: let them but hurry on the marriage, and he'd not quibble about money.

So busy were the ambassadors, so expeditious, that within a few days the contract was signed and sealed. By its terms both bride and groom were to be wed, each by proxy, within ten days of the signing; and in no more than two months thereafter the bride was to be conducted, at her brother's expense, to Abbeville, there to be married at once in her own person to the King himself.

Henry had cause indeed to thank Wolsey; no dipping into his own pockets for a single sou! From the dowry set aside by the bride's father, two hundred thousand gold crowns should be deducted, together with a further two hundred thousand for her trousseau and equipment; the whole four hundred thousand to be paid from the said million crowns owed by France. So Mary should go into France, dowered it would seem with a great sum in gold and a magnificent equipage, but actually with no money at all, and with practically everything she possessed paid for by her groom. The bride who was to bring so much wealth with her brought only paper documents – bills upon France. Mary, herself portionless, was to receive from her husband a portion equal to that of his late Queen Anne who, besides wealth, had brought Brittany as her dower. And more: should he die, whether she chose to live in France or not, Mary was to keep her portion – her revenues, her lands and such gifts as she had received in France, together with all jewels and furnishings she had brought from England.

Certainly Wolsey had done well for his King; and better for himself. Both were jubilant.

Not so the bride. The nearer came the marriage, the deeper grew her repugnance. Wolsey had whispered of non-consummation, but could one trust him? The French King meant to get him a son as soon as might be; and he burned with desire for his bride. As for the promise so soon to be redeemed – who could set bounds to a man's days? . . . and every one of those days a drawn-out misery, and every night a long nightmare.

But, since she looked to her brother to keep his word, she must keep her own. She must show herself a not unwilling bride. She wrote, Wolsey prompting, as was proper to her future husband, showing him all reverence, and all obedience for the marriage-bed. At times she sickened at her own hypocrisy, but what else could she do? Such letters were expected. The groom was a kind old man; was she to shame him with a show of unwillingness? Yet, when she allowed herself to think of the actual bedding, she wished she might die before it came about.

King Henry lost no time; the bargain was too good. Not within the ten days stipulated but in six the proxy marriage took place. On the thirteenth of August, in the state apartments at Greenwich Palace, with those same ceremonies she had been wed to Spain, Mary was wed to France, the proxy-husband being that same Duke of Longueville who had so charmed his King's ears with praises of the bride. The whole court had been invited to witness the proceedings, together with every ambassador save one; the Spanish ambassador, to his own relief, had been forbidden to attend.

The service was to follow the Spanish marriage up to a point. It was to end differently. An act symbolical of putting the bride and groom to bed was to set the validity of this marriage beyond any doubt. Henry was taking no chances. The bride had been prepared; but knowledge of what was to come added to her distress. The act was not only symbolical, it was ridiculous, it was embarrassing. She dreaded it.

The marriage service being finished, Mary withdrew so that her bridal gown be removed for a bedgown such as she wore during her toilet; complete nakedness, as for the marriage-bed, she was spared. Now she was led, accompanied by the Queen and by her ladies-of-honour, into the Presence Chamber where stood the great nuptial bed. Upon this bed, with great ceremony, she was placed, the bedgown being drawn a little aside to show a naked leg. In came the groom with his attendants but he, at least, was fully clothed. A gentleman of the Bedchamber removed one red leather boot and then the hose. Now my lord Duke lay down upon the bed next to the bride; with his own bare leg he touched the bride's and the marriage was declared consummated.

And this she must endure in the presence of the full court; this she must endure beneath the eyes of Charles Brandon. To lie thus, beneath the eyes of the man she loved, shamed her to the very marrow. She lay there red and white by turns.

'I was sick, sick with the shame of it,' she cried out later to Lady Guildford. 'Had I been bedded by the old man himself for all to see, aye, had he taken me as a man takes a woman I had not been so shamed, for the act is less shaming than this foolish play-acting!'

'Comfort yourself,' my lady said. 'It is no mere foolishness; it is a symbol. The taking of the bride by the groom is for the privacy of the marriage chamber. This – that you are pleased, in your ignorance, to call play-acting – is performed in every court of Christendom. None but a green girl would take exception to it.'

But Mary could take no comfort. All that day she remained in her closet and would see no one, not even Catherine the Queen. Nor at night would she appear at the celebrations. Henry made no objection: modesty in a bride is right and proper. But towards midnight, the sounds of revelry having ceased, and the night being moonless by reason of a soft rain falling, she put a cloak about her and walked within the garden. And so walking, she debated within herself whether or no to cast herself into the river and be done with the whole shaming business.

Now while she walked, her feet carrying her towards the river, wretched enough to cast herself therein, but guessing also that life within her ran too strong to consent to her death, she did not hear the soft fall of feet behind her nor know who it was who put his arms around her. She turned herself about within the encircling arms, and seeing that beloved face so close to her own, the face that had seen her shame, she struggled to free herself and run away. But he held her clipped close.

'Why sweetheart!' he cried softly and kissed her full upon the mouth.

'No sweetheart of yours! This day you saw me wedded.'

'But not bedded.'

Again the shame of that ridiculous farce sickened her.

'Wedded or bedded, it is all one. Here we may make an end. Give me my ring again!' And when he shook his head, his hand closing upon his breast where the ring lay, she shrugged. 'Well, keep it or not as you will. No doubt other rings have lain there and will do so again. For me it is no great matter; for now it means nothing. The pledge between us is broken. Into my bed you shall never come! For you pledged your part in today's hateful business. You advised and consented to my marriage. You, yourself; never deny it! You! You!'

He cried out at that and, in spite of herself, she recognized the cry of truth. 'I am the King's well-wisher; and I am my country's well-wisher. And, most of all, I am your own well-wisher! When the King wills a thing, when that thing is for the peace and well-being of his country, when the lady herself consents, what is a man to do? When the King and the bride and the whole Council consents, how shall one man – a man, moreover, whom the King has raised from nothing – refuse? When they put the crown of the Queens of France upon your head' – and now he was bitter indeed – 'you'll forget me soon enough, I promise you!'

'Before that! Before that even!' she cried out, and now she was more bitter than he. 'When they put me in the old man's bed, when the old man himself comes to me, I shall forget everything in the horror of it; everything but this – that to the defilement you consented and played your part.'

'There's nothing could defile you, ever! As for me, again and again you torment me that I consented. What would you have had me do? Speak my useless word and thereafter speak never more? Had you rather they took my head, and sealed in death my tongue and eyes, for me never to speak with you, never to see you again?'

A small anguished sound came from her, like that from a dumb creature nearing its death.

'As it is,' he said, 'we still may set eyes upon each other, touch each other's hand. I shall come into France . . .'

'No!' she cried out, 'never come there! Never come within my sight again. How should I bear it knowing myself bound?'

'But not for *long*. The man is sick and old. We can wait a little. You are young. . . .'

'But *you* are not!' She knew her own cruelty, but could not forbear it. 'You are twice-wed; you can afford to wait for your third marriage. Or, if wait you cannot, there's no less than Madam Margaret, the Archduchess, willing to take you to her bed.'

And when he would have answered, she could not be stopped, but went on trying to ease her pain. 'You have satisfied your needs, taken your pleasure where you found it. But I? I must be put, a virgin, into an old man's bed to find no joy, but disgust, disgust only!' She continued, calmer now, 'Well, we can accustom ourselves to anything; it is our human condition. A wife without love I am, but he'll not know it. A kind wife I shall be and faithful. There is no way but that; or else how shall I face my own soul, how endure my life? Kindliness and duty may overcome disgust – if God be kind!'

'He will be kind . . . to us both. Now he withholds my prize to restore it to me later.'

'You are very sure, my lord!'

'I have good reason. You know well there are two parties at the court . . .'

Yes, she knew that. On one side stood the old nobility; on the other the new men, chief among them Wolsey, the low-born priest, and Brandon, son of a simple squire. Between them the King; and each party trying to pull him their way.

'My party will, for its own sake, help me.'

'Your party does not come into this matter. It is for me to speak. Do not look to have me once I am wed.'

'I would not seek it, save you are free again. I hold your

honour dearer than my own! Had a man so questioned me, he had not lived to ask a second time.'

'For my honour's sake give me my ring again.'

'Not I! You gave it me, and it is mine.'

'Events have changed. Give me my ring!' And she held out her hand.

'Never. No man, nor woman, neither, shall take it from me!' And he placed his hand upon his breast.

'So much for your honour! Well, it is at least well-hid. You are one for safety.' She wounded her own heart with mockery of him. 'And,' she added, wounding her heart still further, 'you are one for your own pleasure also. The Archduchess would be your fourth choice, if I count aright. Oh, I do not count myself. I speak of the little Grey. A child sees clear; she has overmuch sense to take you. As for myself, if the old King dies, never count on me!'

'Mary . . .' He had never called her that name and his speaking of it shook her to the heart's core. 'Not I, but fate gives you to the French King. But here I take my vow: as God hears me, until I bed with you, I'll bed with no woman ever in my life!'

'Then you shall lack a woman all your days – if I may believe you. But believe you I do not. You were never a monk to lack a woman in your life.'

'I do not speak of the past. I speak of what is and what shall be!' He looked at her and it seemed to her all the sorrow of the world lay upon him. And, indeed, now that he had lost her for ever – her heart seeming to be turned from him – he had never found her so desirable. Loss quickened him to her beauty, her sweetness and her honesty; that she was now a queen and more than ever beyond his stars smote him with a deep, an intolerable melancholy. In this moment he loved her deeply, nor would, he truly believed, love any woman again.

'Mary . . .' he said again.

At that speaking of her name her hard pride melted. 'If you will truly swear to take no woman to your bed save me, then I will swear also. To the old man, my husband, I have sworn every wifely duty; I am not one to break my word, nor could I if I would, seeing he marries to get him a son. Yet if he should die – and I wish no one dead – I'll take no man but you. And this I, too, swear before God.' Yet, having said so much, she would not tell him of the promise wrung from the King.

'Why then, I must wait for a dead man's shoes!' And she started that he had read her very thought as though she had spoken aloud. 'It is a hard thing. But our promise, each to the other, stands firm. And so, farewell, my love. . . .'

But not for ever, her heart cried within her breast.

He made to take her in his arms once more; and though she would have given the rest of her life to feel the beat of their two hearts one against the other and the pulsing of all their blood body to body, yet she thrust him aside. 'I am wed and sworn to carry myself as befits a wife,' she reminded him.

'You cannot deny me a last goodbye,' he said.

A last goodbye . . . in spite of her brave words she let him hold her and kiss her. But when he would have gone further than kissing, she tore herself from him. Her duty was to give birth to a true prince for France and not a bastard. She gathered her gown in her two hands and ran from him through the darkness and back to where a few lights glimmered in the house, back to safety and the greater darkness of her own heart.

And now she must style herself Mary, Queen of France. Wolsey, anxious that there should be no slip here as in the marriage with Castile, was continually at her to write with her own hand to the old man, her lord and husband, requesting that he, too, bind himself by proxy marriage, according to his promise. She had no desire to set her hand to such a request, but Wolsey was not a man to be gainsaid, and under his direction she wrote:

To complete the marriage-treaty made between my very dear brother and the most Christian French King, my most beloved husband . . . it is arranged that, after I have contracted marriage by proxy with the said King Louis which I have willingly done on the thirteenth of August, the French King my husband should also contract himself in a like ceremony by a proxy marriage. And I do desire my Lord Earl of Worcester to act as my proxy in France . . .

Wolsey cast a careful eye over what she had written. She spoke French well but her writing of it was not without fault. He corrected an error here and there, waited while she rewrote her letter and sealed it with her new-cut seal – the arms of England and France impaled beneath a crown of *fleur-de-lys*.

On the fourteenth of September King Louis plighted his troth in marriage by proxy to the Earl of Worcester, and by this proceeding Mary was tied by a double knot to the old man she had never seen.

Chapter Seventeen

The Princess of England was now the undoubted Queen of France. There would be no more wars with the French, no more heavy subsidies to pay for them, no more cruel and useless deaths in France. No more calling of gentlemen from their estates or farmers from their fields. In Calais there was even more rejoicing. Their own English Princess was coming into France as its Queen; no longer need they watch the coast nor guard their walls. In France there was the greatest of joy of all. The marriage of their good old King, the father of his people, with the young and beautiful Princess would make him a father indeed! Now there was an end to the fighting, to watching the coast for fear of English attack; and this put paid to Spain, also; without England Spain would never dare. In the streets wine flowed instead of blood; bonfires sprang high and ballads were sung.

In Flanders there was no such rejoicing – the Archduchess had set her heart upon the marriage with Castile; her policies made it desirable. Besides, she missed the man who no longer came backwards and forwards upon that business – Brandon, who had captured her fancy and to whom, God and her father willing, she would gladly give herself.

And now Mary, well and truly wed, must leave for France to make her wedding vows once again before her new subjects with every high ceremony Church and State could devise. To her the high ceremonies presented no difficulties, she enjoyed taking part in them, she enjoyed showing herself to the people. But there would be other, less pleasant duties that filled her with fear and disgust. In the fitting of her splendid gowns, in the jewels and furs laid out for her choice, in the magnificence of the furnishings she should take with her, she tried to forget her hateful obligations.

Though letters went backwards and forwards continually between England and France, Mary herself wrote little to her husband. Sir Thomas Bohier, one of the envoys now returned to France, wrote to her of the King's disappointment.

> . . . The King is sorely grieved that you send him no news of yourself, and also that preparations for the wedding do not go more quickly. Wherefore, Madam, I pray you most humbly to have the goodness to write to him; and I pray you further to do whatever in you lies to come to him as soon as possible, for you can do him no greater pleasure in the world. . . .

Wolsey, too, had received a letter.

'You would swallow the whole fish, Madam, yet strain at a gnat!' he said, striding into her closet where she sat biting upon her quill, the paper blank before her. 'The King your husband deserves better of you. Come now, let me help you.' And so, he dictating, she wrote:

> . . . Very humbly I commend myself to your good grace . . . I have received the letters it has pleased you to write me with your own hand in which I have taken great joy. For which and for the honour it has pleased you to do me, I hold myself forever indebted and obliged to you and thank you as cordially as I can . . . And because you will already have heard how all things move to their conclusion . . .

At the next words she stopped; but, Wolsey repeating them, she wrote:

> . . . and the very especial desire I have to see you and to be in your company . . .

Wolsey said, 'The thing that is worth doing is worth doing well. Is it not a worthy thing to give happiness to a good and kindly old man?'

Well, maybe he was right. But did not one owe something to one's own integrity?

... praying the Creator to give you health and long life,
                         By the hand of your humble ...

'Wife,' said Wolsey. But the gnat, proving overmuch, she wrote instead 'consort'; and signed it with her name.

'Your letter has done good work,' Wolsey said.
'For you, or for me?' Mary asked.
For Wolsey's good work and wisdom in the whole matter he had been made Archbishop of York. Now he carried himself with splendour in fine lawn and rich silk, more clearly – though no more surely – a man to be reckoned with.
'For everyone; but most of all for yourself!' he said very smooth. 'My lord of Worcester has writ that the King your husband has in this world no mind but to pleasure the Queen. Will it please your Grace to hear what he says?' And without waiting for her assent he read aloud:

... The Lord King has provided jewels and goodly gear for her. He has showed me the goodliest and richest sight of jewels that I ever saw. Fifty-six of the greatest diamonds and rubies and also seven of the greatest pearls I have ever seen. And another coffer there was full of goodly girdles, collars, chains, bracelets and other divers jewels. And, merrily laughing, he said My wife shall not have all at once, but at divers times, for he would have many and divers kisses for them ...

The sick look on Mary's face hurried Wolsey on:

... He thinks every hour a day till he sees her. He is never well but when he hears speech of her. I make no doubt she will have a good life with him by the grace of God ...

Hard upon this letter followed the groom's gift. Wolsey and Henry brought her the jewel together.
'Foretaste of what is to come,' Wolsey said, bowing and smiling.
Foretaste of what I must give ... for this thing how many kisses? Yet even she must look upon the great jewel with amazement.

It was an ornament for neck and bosom; a diamond of purest water as large and broad as a man's forefinger, set about with pearls and, pendant therefrom, a pear-shaped pearl as large as a pigeon's egg. Henry's eyes gleamed with desire. He took it in his hand and could scarce endure to give it back again.

'Now you must wear it,' Wolsey said. 'That all Christendom knows how you honour the lord your husband and his gift.'

Henry's valuation was more practical. He commanded the jewellers of Jeweller's Row to the Palace to speak as to the jewel's worth. They were of one mind. It was worth – if such another might be found again – at the very least eighty thousand gold crowns.

Henry could be generous to madness when he had the mind. First to show his own magnificence, thereafter to pleasure his sister, he showed that pleasing madness now. Page upon page listed the goods that were to go with the bride.

A battalion of craftsmen sat and sewed her gowns beneath the eyes of four master-tailors of Paris. There were sixteen dresses of the most costly stuffs stitched in raised patterns of gold or silver, and sewn with jewels, and a bridal gown of white cloth-of-gold sewn all with diamonds. These Henry had commanded to be cut in the French style – as before he had commanded them to be cut in the style of the Netherlands. The French gowns were lower in the neck than any Mary had ever worn; she flushed crimson when she saw her nakedness in the looking-glass. 'Nay, never blush,' my lady Guildford said. 'The great jewel shall hide a good deal.' And since the French King bore the title Duke of Milan, there were six gowns cut in the Italian style, whose great skirts were not equally full all round but flat in front and fuller than the English style at side and back. And, since her own England must make good showing, there were eight gowns in English fashion, and these for their dear familiar look she liked best of all. There were collars of finest lace, petticoats of rich silks and stays of satin laced all of gold. There were mantles, there were coats, there were hoods for all occasions.

There were caskets overflowing with jewels, there were

necklaces and girdles, bracelets and rings, jewelled garters and shoe-buckles, jewelled combs and hair-pins. There were her two new seals – the great seal of silver engraved with the arms of England and France, and her privy seal of gold engraved with a crown and four roses. There were chests of plate, including one of pure gold set with sapphire and pearl for great occasions. There was plate for her private chapel, altar-cloths and hangings of fine-stitched tapestries. There were chairs and stools and chests for her bedchamber, all carved by a master's hand. There were coaches and horses and attendants in the Queen's new livery. There were banners of saints and banners for her litters bearing the arms of her father, her mother and grandfather Edward IV. There was a canopy of Estate in azure silk, stitched with the figure of Our Lord sitting on a rainbow, and worked in gold about the hanging sides of the canopy with her own motto, *La Volunté de Dieu me suffit.*

She saw all these treasures as from a distance. They had nothing to do with her. They went as part of a bargain in which she had had no word. She was forced less to God's will than to her brother's; and her own will did not consent thereto.

Between her fears for the future, the fitting of her gowns and the choosing of her jewels and furs, she must learn not only the etiquette of the French court – together with the names of those who had influence therein – but also she must better herself in the French tongue. Some French she had; it was impossible to be brought up in her brother's court without a working knowledge of it. She spoke easily but not without fault; the rules were beyond her. Her pride would not allow her to speak less well than she might; Dr John Palsgrave wrote a French grammar for her – the first French grammar ever to have been written and for many years the only French grammar.

Every ship from France brought her presents from her

groom; presents of such richness that Henry's eyes – those small blue eyes – gleamed. But for Mary every gift brought back the words of the old King; the idea of doling out kisses for every gift made, or to be made, sickened her. She longed for fleeting time to slacken or to stop altogether. Every tide brought letters from her old husband – to herself, to Wolsey, to the King, bidding them haste, haste; he burned with desire to set eyes upon his wife, to clasp her to his heart.

One comfort she did have. Lady Guildford was truly a mother these days; loving and understanding. She warned, she advised, she comforted – as far as comfort was possible; above all, she promised that death alone would part her from the darling child she had nurtured.

In early September, the wind blowing razor-keen, and a needle-sharp rain falling, Mary rode out in high procession to leave the country she loved for the country she feared. The King, the Queen and the full court rode with her; and, as they rode, from every house and cottage the people came flocking to bid her Godspeed; and she that desired nothing more than to weep must keep a gracious smiling face. She had not wanted Catherine to attend her for the Queen was near to her time, but 'How else may I show my love?' she asked.

'By staying quiet at home and presenting me with my nephew,' Mary told her.

'I could not scant affection to my sweet sister, nor courtesy to the Queen of France,' Catherine said.

And so, the weather growing yet worse, they reached Dover Castle, standing high and exposed to bleak wind and rain; and there they must remain while an English autumn did its worst. Never within living memory had the folk of Dover seen the seas so rough, so high, the fierce winds lashing the water into such fury. Once, well wrapped about, Mary, standing upon the ramparts, saw a wrecked ship break in pieces, saw the small black figures that were struggling vainly in the water cast up on the beach. She came within to put up a prayer for their souls. A few days later two more wrecks were cast upon the coast; even when the weather lightened a little she dare not walk lest she see the pitiful bodies, unrested, troubled, stiff in death.

October came in. On the second day of the month, in the dark of the morning, Mary was aroused from sleep by a knocking upon the door. In the room beyond she heard her women busy about some work.

'Madam,' Lady Guildford told her, 'the wind has dropped and the sea is calm. With God's blessing we may catch a glimpse of the sun this day. You must haste and dress! Your women are about your packing, and the ships are making ready.'

She said not a word but allowed them to make her ready and then down she went where, in the chill of the early morning, the King and Queen and the whole court waited to bid her farewell. One by one, those who were leaving her came to kneel, to kiss her hand. The King's sharp eyes watched as Brandon knelt; her pale face showed no further emotion. It is the end, he thought, to all their nonsense. . . .

It is the end . . . the end . . . Mary's heart echoed.

The King took her hand to lead her from the castle; and now, noticing her pallor and the fear darkening her eyes, he whispered, 'I have not forgotten my promise.' At which her pale lips smiled, but the words seemed now to belong to the world of fantasy.

The morning had promised too fair; they had done better to wait before trusting to the treachery of its early calm. Scarce had she set foot within the ship, when the wind rose again and the sea with it. The high winds buffeting the ships separated them; some were driven to Flanders, others to Calais. 'We'll not need to fear pirates,' said the captain, seeing the dark heaving sea all about them. 'It must be bold pirates, indeed, that would dare this weather!'

It was still the dark of the morning when Mary's ship was cast upon a sandbank of a fair-sized town, and there it remained fast.

'What is the town?' Mary asked, as she lay seasick, longing for death.

'Boulogne, Madam,' she was told; and she thanked God she had not been delivered into the hands of the Netherlands.

So there, the boat rocking still in the unquiet water, there was safety at last. And now came dear Mother Guildford together with some ladies to look to the Queen's comfort. They brought her wine and bread; they sponged her face and hands; they combed the tangles of her hair, leaving it free-flowing as becomes a virgin bride, and they changed her gown soiled with sea-water and seasickness.

They might have spared their pains. In Abbeville, the King of France waited, all impatience for his bride; and a King must not be kept waiting even by his Queen. So into an open boat she was lowered; and, the waves still high and breaking over her waist-deep, she surrendered herself again to seasickness. And still the waves dashed higher, so that it was God's wonder the boat did not overturn. Yet still Mary might not step ashore; the boat which could have beached in shallow water dared not, for there was no strip of land upon which they might set foot. Then one of her retinue who was taller than most men, went into the water and carried her in his arms through the dashing waves, to set her down upon this foreign soil.

'You were indeed a piteous sight,' Lady Guildford told her later. 'Your face was white as the foam and no man could guess the colour of your hair, for it was dark with water; no, nor the colour of your eyes for they were fast shut. And all those that had come down to welcome you cried out, lamenting that the waves had brought them a dead Queen!'

At Boulogne they were forced to rest, and there they heard that King Henry's great flagship, his newest and proudest, that had been sent for her especial protection, had been broken by the storm and lost together with five hundred men. So fresh and fearful a disaster, the loss of the great ship and so many who were to have ridden with the Queen to her marriage but had gone down instead into the waters, filled them all with deep sorrow.

The next day, the Duke of Valois sent asking that he might wait upon his Queen; and she must, in the mood or no, receive him. So in he came, a gallant young man that bowed himself to the very ground, as to a goddess, no less.

'Madam,' he said, 'I bring you the most loving greetings from my master, the lord King your husband. He cannot contain his desire to see you and wed you in his own person.'

At that last, she heard a small smothered laugh as from one who felt she must, yet could not, contain herself. It came from a girl on the verge of womanhood, one of her own ladies whom she did not know; a thin girl, sallow, with a longish nose and great dark eyes. She had a profusion of dark curls and a very red mouth, a mouth she was biting now in her effort not to laugh. The idea of the old man panting for his young mate she clearly found amusing.

Mary ignored the laughter; she misliked even the noting of such ill-behaviour. Later she asked who the girl might be.

'It is Mistress Anne Bullen,' Lady Guildford told her. 'You must forgive her manners; she is come of jumped-up stock on the one side. Her great-grandfather was but a merchant – and a pretty shrewd one judging from the money he made and the noble wife his son married. Her mother's mother was daughter of the Earl of Surrey; her uncle, Lord Thomas Howard, married the Lady Anne Plantagenet. She is, she announces it far and wide, your own cousin! But the vulgar streak will out!'

'I did not choose her; how comes she here?'

'The lord King added her to your list of ladies – partly to please his friend Surrey, partly because she is merry and quick of her laughing . . . too quick, it would seem. And young though she is, she can sing a song, playing the while upon her lute. He thought to make you merry with her company.'

'She is over-merry for my company. I do not like this young lady who knows not how to conduct herself in the presence of the Queen of France. Bid her carry herself with more respect.'

It was a full and glorious procession that rode for Abbeville. First came two thousand English men-at-arms well mounted, and two hundred bowmen, riding also; and all of them in Tudor colours of green and white that made the autumn countryside blossom as though it were spring. Next came some hundred gentlemen, headed by England's chief peers, each riding with a Frenchman of his own estate. Following them, upon a white steed trapped all in green and silver, came Mary, like sweet May, in a gown of white cloth-of-silver and a short coat of cloth-of-gold; with, upon her fair hair flowing free, a cap that blazed with jewels.

Behind her rode thirty ladies headed by Lady Guildford, the last and least being the pert Anne Bullen, all attired in crimson velvet; one hundred archers, all in green, rode with them as bodyguard. Now followed the empty litter of the Queen, all hung with cloth-of-gold stitched with *fleurs-de-lys*, and hard upon it her three coaches, two hung with cloth-of-gold and one in crimson velvet, all bearing the arms of England and France intertwined, and each drawn by six matching horses, all of white. Last came the long line of wagons, carrying chests of gowns, of jewels and furs, of plate, tapestries and furnishings for the Queen's rooms and for her private chapel.

Chapter Eighteen

Within a dozen miles from Abbeville they were met by a
great procession headed by the chief peers of France; leading
them was Francis of Valois, Count of Angoulême, Duke of
Savoy, son-in-law to the King and heir-apparent to the throne.
A very fine young man, handsome and upright, slender of
waist and broad of shoulder; her brother, Mary thought,
would have envied those well-turned legs. His hazel eyes were
quick and bright, his mouth sensitive and sensual, his nose
somewhat long; but in a man that matters little – save he
bequeath it to his daughters. She approved his magnificent
clothes which he wore with distinction, and his jewels; the
earring in one ear she thought a delightful and delicate piece
of frivolity. He was all man for a proper woman. She thought
if she must wed royal France then this should have been her
man. He could pleasure any woman in bed; she had done
better with him than with the old sick man whose days were
numbered.

The eyes of these two met. She thought with this man I
could be happy. I love Brandon, but between us the deep sea
rolls and I think I shall never see him again. I shall keep him
in my heart for ever; not so much as a man but as a bright
dream. But life is to be lived as it is. With this man, this
Francis, I could have married and borne a King of France . . .
but that, too, is a dream. . . .

The bright and lively eyes, meeting her own, dropped; a
fine jewelled hand passed over them then, as though, sun-
dazzled, he must shield them from the sight of unendurable
beauty.

'Madam,' he said and stopped. He could not bring himself to utter the second title of his ceremonial greeting – mother. For the fair young girl, wed to his wife's father, was, by the law of kinship, his also – and he two years or so her senior. A pity he had not waited, a pity circumstances had forced him to marry the child Claude, fourteen and her eyes still wet from the death of her mother, even though he had gained Brittany with her. Already he had consoled himself with Diane de Poitiers, a fine upstanding young woman who washed in rainwater every day and looked splendid as a new-blown rose. But this girl who was now his mother-in-law was a bud to unfold in the warmth of a man's love – and with her he might have secured England, if Henry VIII had no child. And he could have kept himself faithful . . . at any rate until the rose was overblown.

When, the words of courtesy and loving friendship spoken, he had taken himself away and she had withdrawn into her closet, Lady Guildford said, 'This Duke is the nonpareil of princes. He loves painters and musicians and carvers in stone; he encourages them and pays them freely that they may live while they work . . .'

'He loves women also,' put in Anne Bullen, 'and has no need to pay them for their services. And can you wonder? His wife is plain and brown and of a most shocking virtue!'

'You could do with some of that same virtue yourself!' Lady Guildford told her, very sharp. And, seeing the girl in no way abashed, but with a look in her dark eye as though she could teach my lady more than a little about men, the Queen said, 'Mistress, you would do well to watch your tongue. Loose speech, though it be in jest, may hurt others; but be sure, in the end, it will come back to hurt yourself. Let us hear no more of such talk – or home you shall go, and double-quick!'

Now, her reproof given, Mary wished to turn the talk to pleasanter matters. She had noticed that, whatever the occasion, the girl wore a riband about her long throat.

'Mistress,' she said, 'you introduce a new fashion – a riband about your neck . . .' and stopped short. For a dull red had spread over the sallow cheeks.

'It is a pretty fashion,' said she, a little defiant.

'A bare neck upon a young maid is prettier,' Mary said; and then added for no reason at all, save that she liked on occasion to be precise, 'So the neck be unspotted.'

The red deepened in the girl's cheeks.

Later Lady Guildford told the Queen, 'She has some blemish, they say; a wart or mole upon the neck that she hides beneath her riband.'

'I cannot blame her. And it is, as she says, a pretty fashion.'

'It may be an unkind tale. She is not much liked. She's very proud, and can be spiteful with it. As for what the riband hides, I do not know. I have never seen it. But what I have seen, and no doubt the Queen has, also – she has a small swelling at the base of each little finger, as though another finger budded.'

'I have not noticed it.'

'She's clever there, too! She covers it with a wide sleeve of her own devising; it falls to the knuckles.'

'Another pretty fashion: I have noticed it – and equally successful. Wart and budding flesh! She does well to hide them. Simple blemishes; yet more than one has hanged for them!'

Lady Guildford nodded. 'Many hold them for witchmarks; and in this case they'd not be far wrong. The girl's a witch. Young though she is – and no beauty neither – she can bewitch any man she chooses.'

'I'll have no scandals! Let her play her tricks – and home she goes in disgrace: I'd not be sorry. I cannot like her!'

'Nor can the most part of ladies. Who can stomach the woman that can – and will if she please – steal her husband from his wife's very bed!'

'There's some ladies would give her thanks for that!' the Queen said.

The great procession crawled on; and always the folk cheered and cried out their blessings – blessings she thought she should need. A mile and a half from Abbeville a procession of riders drew up to meet them. 'It is the lord King himself,' Duke Francis whispered. 'He could not wait, it seems, for the sight of you!' And he slackened his speed to fall in behind her and make place for the King.

She bowed to the saddle, lowering her eyes less from modesty than in panic. Beneath her half-closed lids she saw a frail old man, yellow, bent and sickly. Yet, in spite of that, her heart a little lightened. He was not the disease-bloated, monstrous-headed creature that had been rumoured. Nothing but a tired, kind old man; and the head, though shaking a little, not unworthy of a crown – for the seal once set is set for ever. *But he is old and cold and mouldy-smelling as the grave; and with this corpse I must bed.* Yet, even with this thought running ratlike in her mind, she knew her duty. She made as though to dismount to greet him in due form; but the golden armour of her gown restrained her. And he, for all the dullness of his eye, understood and put out a hand to prevent her. He did not offer to dismount; it had not been proper in a King, but he brought his horse alongside and leaned across and saluted her full upon the lips. And she was right. His kiss was indeed churchyard cold, smelling of the grave. Yet she took it with such grace and sweetness, that at this meeting of their lips such a tumult of cheering went up that it seemed the heavens themselves must crack and splinter.

They rode a few paces together, he telling her that, unable to wait for the sight of his bride, he had, under pretence of hawking, ridden out with fifteen hundred gentlemen. But who rides ahawking with fifteen hundred gentlemen? It was enough to scare the birds for miles around.

Still leaning across his mare's neck he said, 'Now I ride back to Abbeville. I want my Queen to take the people's eye herself, herself alone, without the King to share her glory. For her and her alone the greetings, the homage and the prayers. Within two hours or three we shall expect you!'

And away he went, bent over his horse, riding careful as the old must do.

Rest she could not, nor eat either. Now she was over her first relief that her husband was no monster, resentment burned in her that to serve their policies they had thrust her into an old man's bed. Back she came into the little church and knelt to pray.

'All your praying will not help' – warned Duke Francis, who had followed on silent feet and stood behind her – 'unless your own goodwill does its part. Show kindness to the old man and it shall be repaid a thousandfold.'

For how long? How long before she put aside the bridal veil, before she donned her widow's weeds? And until that time . . . what then? The question beat in both heads; they sighed, each of them, that Francis had not waited. In the thought she felt no wrong. If she must wed to unite their two countries then, with sorrow for her lost love but with no crawling of the flesh upon her bones, how willing would she have bedded with this handsome Duke! And he? He coveted her sweet flesh and, one way or another, meant to have it.

About five o'clock of the autumn evening the procession halted outside the walls of Abbeville. At the Marcade Gate, the Queen dismounted and stepped into the golden litter patterned with the lilies of France; the curtains had been drawn back and the cushions set high so that she might be well seen by all; and so, to the sound of five hundred trumpets answered by the martial sound of guns within, she entered the city. The autumn light, grown somewhat dim, the city had gained in splendour. By the door of every house stood a citizen holding a flaring torch; and so, trumpets and guns answering each other, the procession passed under triumphal arches through streets all hung with tapestries and green garlands. No Queen could have had a more glorious welcome, as Mary came to the King's lodging, the Gruthuse Palace.

In an anteroom the Duke of Norfolk, waiting to conduct her to the King, saw her eyes wide with terror and said, 'Be of good courage, Madam. The King has a most gentle spirit; you have nothing to fear.'

She tried to smile at that, wondering at his man's ignorance. Even when a woman loves a man, and even though she be no longer a virgin, still her heart must beat faster at his coming ... and in that beating is fear. How then must it be with an untried virgin, her heart already given, soon to be put into an old man's bed?

And now, seeing her pale as any lily, my lady Guildford came to brush a little colour on her cheeks, and to set the fair hair upon her shoulders. My lady lifted the train, and my lord of Norfolk taking her by the hand, she suffered them to lead her into the Presence Chamber.

Used she was to goodly sights, both at her brother's court and at her father's also; but neither at her brother's wedding nor at his crowning had she seen a room so splendidly adorned, or so vast, so shining a concourse, arranged within the frame of the splendid room as it might be a picture. This was *her* court; and she was its Queen.

She made her deep obeisance to the King, and did not, as etiquette ruled, look him in the face. The Duke of Norfolk put out a hand to raise her to her feet; but from the great chair the King himself stepped down and kissed her upon both cheeks and then full on the mouth. It was, she thought, like a dry leaf falling light and empty of life. It was in no way offensive ... but it was not a kiss for a young bride to take from her groom. He led her to a lesser chair beside his own, and the Duke of Norfolk delivered his King's greetings of brotherly love, whereat Louis answered in words no one could catch, his voice being frail as his person. Then Francis, Duke of Valois, Count of Angoulême, heir-apparent to the throne, came from his place by the King. Kissing both her hands he said, his young man's voice clear and true, 'Since I cannot myself go to our brother the King of England, I send my heart to him with this promise: I am at his service. I will serve him – my own gracious King permitting – in his wars against any prince in Christendom.'

'Sir,' she told him, 'I thank you with all my heart, both for myself and for my brother the King of England also.' But for all that she knew it was not love for England that had spoken in him, but hatred for Spain and the Netherlands. It was, indeed, little less than a veiled threat against these countries. But, whatever the motive, the offer, if he truly meant to stand by it, was worth very much to England. She could understand now her brother's desire for this marriage.

Now the old man, slowly rising, gave her his hand; a hand so weak, so fragile it could scarce support the weight of her small and light fingers. He led her, followed by his high peers, into the banqueting hall. Seated in her place by the King, she looked about for her English friends; seeing no familiar face, she wondered where they might be. Madam the Princess Claude, who stood behind her chair, whispered that Duke Francis had taken the English ambassadors, together with the English peers, to dine in his own palace. Now, surrounded by foreign, unknown faces, she felt lost indeed.

The King ate sparingly; one might say, she thought, he played with his food. His face was forever turned to his bride, as though he could never be done looking at her; and all the time he paid her this compliment and that; or asked her questions from which, short as she might make her answers, his attention wandered. Look at him she must, and liked no better what she saw. He was thin as a bone and bleached as a bone; scant grey hair straggled beneath the jewelled bonnet, and the eyes between red lids and dark sagging pouches were those of an old man wearied to his death. His mouth was scarce to be distinguished from the rest of his face, so pale it was, so thin, so without shape; nor could she imagine what shape it might have been, so slack it was for lack of teeth. His shoulders were hunched, his head bent so that he might the better see his food, and his fingers so brittle she wondered he could handle it at all. But when he smiled she began to glimpse the young man he might have been. Always he would have been thin and round of shoulder, but there would have been a brightness in the eye and a sweetness in the mouth to match his kindliness. So now, for pride in herself and some pity for him, she leaned to him, smiling and laughing and flashing at him the bright sparks of her mirth. And, so strangely are we made that, acting her part, she for a little while forgot her pretence, and for that brief moment her sorrows and fears.

The feasting over, she was led by a watchful Lady Guildford to a retiring room to rest and to refresh her person before the great ball that was to follow. How gladly would she have taken to rest in bed – so she had that bed to herself. When Duke Francis came to lead her to the dancing, she found the great hall had been cleared, though the smell of baked meats lingered still. The old man sat in his high place set about with cushions; the courtiers standing in due order – upon one side the ladies, upon the other the gentlemen.

She moved, Duke Francis at her side, up the aisle of curtseying courtiers, but when she herself would have curtseyed to the King, his trembling hand forbade it; on slow uncertain feet, he stepped down to take her hand. The company now having moved to make a circle about the room, the King made to lead her in the dance; but after a few steps the death-like pallor of his face, the beads upon his forehead and the short panting of his breath sounded their warning. He gave her into the hands of Duke Francis and allowed himself to be led to the great cushioned chair in which he sat for the rest of the evening, looking upon the dancers with a kindly fatherly eye.

Duke Francis would have danced yet another measure with his King's delightful bride, but she knew her duty. There were others, both French and English, who must share that honour; a man overlooked is a man with a grievance. Such grievances, she knew well, could flame into sudden quarrel; and such quarrels, given time and opportunity, set a whole realm alight. Between dances she went to sit by the King to receive the chief lords and ladies of France.

With the Princess Claude, daughter of the old King and wife to Duke Francis, she talked at some length, the Princess seated upon a stool at her feet. With her sad, dark face, her sombre gown, her quiet assured manner and her thickened figure, for she was already pregnant, she looked, young as she was, a woman to be reckoned with.

The ball came to a short halt while the old King tottered from his throne and was taken off to bed. His usual time to retire was six o'clock but in honour of the occasion he had outstayed his time by some hours. He dined, Mary heard with some dismay, at eight o'clock in the morning; she hoped to win him to the more reasonable hour of twelve. As for his bedtime, so long as he did not expect her to accompany him, she was more than pleased for him to retire at his unusual time; she was used to dancing till the early hours, nor did she ever think of retiring until midnight. He did not expect this festivity, at least, to come to an early end. At the door he paused and made a sign for the dancing to continue.

At dawn Mary was led by Duke Francis and followed by her ladies along a covered gallery set for her especial comfort between the King's lodgings and her own; for the old man, with loving care, would not have her walk this October night through the dew-wet gardens that lay between the Gruthuse Palace and her own apartments. There the Duke, clearly unwilling, made his adieux and Mary was put to bed. 'Sleep well, Madam!' my lady Guildford said; and the Queen caught a whisper, low but clear, 'Let her take her chance to sleep while she may!' Who spoke the words she did not know, but the high-pitched laugh of the Bullen girl she knew only too well.

But Mary lay unsleeping. The face of Brandon rose clear before her – this, this was the man she truly loved. Her heart reproached her that she could, for one moment, consider any other – even Duke Francis.

She tossed and turned and sighed and wept into her pillow until Lady Guildford, hearing her restless movements, came in, a bedgown on her, with a cup of wine. She stirred the embers and set the wine to warm; she placed a stool by the bed and listened to her lady's self-reproaching doubts, but talk of Duke Francis she dismissed out of hand. 'Oh, the Duke has

146

a fine bearing, a good wit and an open purse! Every friend, every poet, painter or music-maker finds him generous – to a point only. He gives but he expects a good return. He's gay and courteous and kind . . . to the eye. But scratch him a little and there's the true man – wayward and weak-willed, selfish and hard. The old King is, believe it, Madam, the better bargain. Be glad you are not wed to the Duke. He's broken many a woman's heart, and will no doubt break many more. But not his wife's heart, though he may make it ache. The Princess Claude is strong. Because she is no beauty she has learned her lesson and learned it well. He does not know how much he needs her. But she knows. She loves him and gives him his head, lets him sleep with his women and beget his bastards; but it is she that carries the Duke's true heir and that heir may be the next King . . . unless, Madam, you do your duty. And it is a duty you must make haste about, for the King is old . . .'

'I have no wish to bear a child for France. My sole wish is to go home and wed my love!'

'It is not a Christian woman's wish . . .'

'It is a true woman's wish; and it is *my* wish!'

Lady Guildford could find nothing she might answer to that; she picked up the wine-cup and went quietly away.

Chapter Nineteen

Mary awoke in the strange room to the sound of the joyful clangour of bells and wondered where she might be. It was Sunday, the bells told her so. But, memory flooding back, it came to her wretched heart that these were wedding-bells; her own wedding-bells. And the day was not Sunday, it was Monday; it was the ninth of October. It was St Denis's Day; St Denis, the patron saint of France, had been chosen to bless her marriage.

A knock sounded upon her door and in came Lady Guildford carrying wine, fresh rolls, honey and butter. Mary had eaten little the previous day; now, wretched and fearful as she was, she fell to, and was all the better for the good food.

Now came her women to bathe her and brush her; to oil her and to paint her; but for her painting she had today made a pale bride. Now came Lady Guildford carrying the bridal robe. Mary had dressed all her life in gowns befitting her station, yet even she, though it had been fitted and pinned upon her in person, had not remembered its full magnificence. It was of cloth-of-gold; not that heavy armoured material in which she had first greeted her lord, but a very fine tissue sewn thick with diamonds patterned in roses and lilies that glittered and blazed. The low neck was furred with ermine and ermine lined the great sleeves hanging to the ground and the sweeping fluted hem.

Into this gown she was laced and then, a towel about her shoulders, her loosened hair was powdered with gold lest the gown dim its paler brilliance. Then – she shining gold from hair to shoes – the royal mantle of purple velvet lined with ermine was put about her shoulders. And now that she was all decked and ready, in came the Duke of Norfolk and her kinsman the Earl of Dorset to lead her to the sacrifice. Before them walked a small page, very fair and much curled, who bore upon a scarlet cushion a coronet of rare craftsmanship, set with great gems, that gathered into itself all the sunlight of the October day and held the light so that it glowed like the sun.

'The lord King sends this jewel to Madam the Queen and he bids me say, "None but the fairest lady may wear such a jewel; and such a jewel deserves none but the fairest neck in France."' Mary the Queen sent her thanks to the most gracious King, scarce knowing what words she said; and then stood statue-still while the blazing coronet was set upon her head. And though she knew that she was well-favoured, Mary stared astonished at the reflection in the looking-glass held before her. The tall, slight figure in gold and ermine, the fair glittering hair spread upon her shoulders, with, above it, the marvellous coronet. But the eyes, the frightened eyes, showed her to be all too human.

It being now past eight-thirty, and the ceremony timed for nine o'clock, she must leave her closet. Before her walked twenty-six knights, two by two; then followed two heralds and two gentlemen carrying maces. The Duke of Norfolk gave her his arm, and upon her other side walked her cousin Dorset. Behind her came Lady Guildford leading the Queen's ladies, thirteen in number, each one between two gentlemen who carried, each, a plumed bonnet in his hand. Very pretty they looked, these young creatures, bright eyes downcast, lashes sweeping rosy cheeks, in their wedding gowns of cloth-of-silver, with sashes of Tudor green upon the shoulder. As they came to the great doorway, the English lords who had been waiting fell into place; and, my lady Guildford holding up the Queen's train, the procession came into the street, for today there was to be no passing through any contrived gallery; the crowds were to have full sight of their Queen. Lining each side of the road stood English bowmen all in new suits of green; the people might come so far but no farther.

The great hall of the Gruthuse Palace had been furnished like a church since in Abbeville there was none large enough to hold the vast congregation. It was a chamber noble enough for any royal occasion; the ceiling carved and gilded, the stained-glass windows casting rich lights upon the floor of mosaic cunningly devised. The walls hung now with fine tapestries.

Upon a raised dais, the cloth of Estate held aloft by Francis, Duke of Valois, and the Duke of Alençon, sat the royal groom attended by the Archbishop of Rouen and the Bishop of Amiens and, glorious in their robes of gleaming crimson silk, the Cardinals of Brie and Bayeux; behind him stood his chief nobles and the foreign ambassadors. In the great throne the old man blazed in cloth-of-gold, bejewelled and befurred, with, shining upon his breast, the order of St Michael. The glittering cloth-of-gold drained every sign of life from him; he was yellow-grey as a corpse, every imperfection of age exaggerated. The old hands, thin and fragile as birds' claws, lay pitiful upon the shining folds of his gown . . . an old, old man with the face of a corpse.

As the Queen entered the great doorway the trumpets sounded; and she, like a dead woman walking, moved the length of the hall and came to the foot of the dais. The old man stirred, doffed his bonnet; the Queen curtseyed down to the ground. The King rose slowly to his feet and held out his hand; she rose and he kissed her full upon the mouth. Then came the Treasurer, Robertat, with the King's marriage gift – a necklace of gold upon which hung a great pear-shaped diamond some two inches long, together with a diamond of like size of purest colour. The old man bent to fasten it about her neck. Then, she standing, he kissed her again upon the mouth.

So they stood side by side, the eighteen-year-old bride and the groom with his burnt-out, wasted and sick body. The contrast between them was painful; impossible save that it was there, not to be denied by any eye.

Nine o'clock cast its stroke upon the air. . . . She would remember always counting one, two, three . . . and then losing count. She would remember always the cardinals' scarlet robes and the bishops' gold-stitched copes and jewelled mitres; and she would remember how she had thought the old man to be more bearable had his gown not been that of a young man, but dark and more suited to his years.

She heard the high sweet singing of the boy choristers and the voices, deep and impersonal, of the cardinals reciting the High Mass; young voices and old voices intoning prayers, and now the unfamiliar words of the marriage service and her own voice, assenting, promising . . . promising. She felt nothing; neither sorrow nor despair, nor even bitterness. She was an empty vessel making a sound. She felt the great ring put upon her finger; felt that kiss, dry and light as a withered leaf. She felt the old thin hand within her own. As in a dream she had been wed. But it was no dream; it was a reality beyond all escaping, save death released her; death alone.

And now came the ceremony of the offerings. At the high altar Duke Francis, kneeling, held a great Bible opened flat upon his knee; the Duke of Alençon knelt by him holding a bag of gold pieces. Between them stood the King. Slowly the old hands dipped into the bag; one by one the gold pieces were lifted and laid upon the great open book, covering both pages in a high glittering heap. And, the bag being emptied, Monseigneur the Cardinal de Brie, walking slow and careful, laid the shining weight of the Bible before the high altar. Now came the Princess Claude carrying also a great bag of purple velvet upon a cushion. She knelt upon both knees giving it into the Queen's hands. And seeing her humbly kneeling, Mary remembered that the late Queen was but nine months dead, and that this her daughter, her young bereaved daughter, must now kneel to a new Queen.

Claude raised her eyes, large and sorrowful. She smiled, she smiled at the interloper. It was a smile to win Mary for ever. She wanted to cry out, 'It is none of my doing. I, too, am forced . . .' Her hand moved upon the cushion to touch that of the kneeling girl. The girl gave no sign; only knelt there with her sorrowful eyes and her faint-smiling mouth. Yet of that touch affection and trust were born. Mary heard her own thoughts very clear: *Here is honesty, here is kindliness, here is true nobility. This is the one to cherish as my friend . . .*

And now it was time for the feast; and she, their new young Queen, must entertain the Princesses of the Blood at her own table.

So down she went to face the ordeal, for she was woman enough to know that in a strange land women are less generous than men. 'Women are aye the worst,' Lady Guildford echoed the Queen's thoughts, 'for they will kneel and bow and scrape and speak very humble; but the thoughts of their hearts they keep close until the occasion be fitting to let them loose. And then, wounding as an arrow, they let fly!'

'It is not true of the Princess Claude; she is honest as the day. She is sorrowful, as is natural, seeing me in her mother's place, and that mother so late dead. But she is royal every way. She knows her *devoir* and will perform it to the uttermost. Honesty at a King's court is a jewel to be treasured, and I value her friendship above rubies!' She fingered the jewel at her neck wondering if it had been worn by Anne of Brittany, Claude's mother.

In the dining-chamber tables were set out with fine cloths. Lamps hung from the walls, candles shed their softer light upon gold plate, upon ships and towers cunningly fashioned and carrying spices. Beneath a cloth of Estate the Queen's great chair was set, and as Mary came to her place the Princess Claude knelt to serve the Queen. But Mary would have none of it; she raised the kneeling girl to put her in the place of honour at her own right hand; Lady Guildford sat at the Queen's left. As to the latter, it was a kindly act and natural, for my lady had been to the Queen as a mother; but it was not according to etiquette. Princesses of the Blood came first. It is not wise to flout etiquette, even if one be a Queen – especially if one be a Queen. The setting of Lady Guildford in so high a place caused much jealous talk.

The feasting at length being over, they repaired into the great hall of the Gruthuse Palace now made ready for the purpose – to continue the merrymaking. The King took his seat in the great chair upon the dais, but this time he made no attempt to lead the Queen in the dance. Once more Duke Francis took his place; his manner was one of extreme respect, but there was that in his eye that bespoke more than respect.

And now, it being eight of the clock, and for the King the hour very late, he came shakily from his chair to retire to his closet. But still the Queen cried out for another dance and yet another, until the message came. The King awaited his bedding.

So she must allow herself to be led, not to her lodgings but to the Queen's closet hard by the King's; and there she was stripped, one by one, first of her Queen's robes, and then of her woman's clothing, until she stood naked. Then, a bedgown about her, she was led into the Queen's bedroom; it was the duty of the Princess Claude, Madam of France, to strip the Queen of her bedgown and lead her to the nuptial bed. Even in her own appalling fear, Mary pitied the girl that must put another woman in her mother's bed. Following them came the French Princesses and the Queen's ladies, the last couple being two very young women – the one Anne Bullen, and the other a little older, whom Mary scarce noticed save that she was full-breasted and very handsome.

Madam Claude and Lady Guildford turned back the covering of velvet embroidered with the arms of France and England intertwined, and put the Queen into the great bed where, for all the warmth of braziers burning, she shivered. And, lying there, every sense sharpened, she heard a smothered word from those two who had brought up the rear, and knew well that they laughed, whispering that soon she should be warm enough.

Now came the sound of footsteps and in they came, the Duke Francis and the Duke of Alençon, bringing in the groom followed by the high peers of France. In the great folds of his bedgown he looked leaner than ever; as though, were it not for the girdle knotted about him, he must slip through the folds and be forever lost. But when the knot was untied and the gown taken from him she had to shut her eyes against the sight of him . . . the yellowish skin, the sparse grey hairs and the signs of his lost virility. Mercifully, her closed eyes were taken as a sign of virgin modesty; yet she knew well that the whole company – some shocked, some maliciously amused – noted well the difference between groom and bride; knew also that not one woman of them all, even the oldest, envied her her groom.

And now the Bishop of Amiens brought the nuptial cup of wine from which the man they called her husband must first drink, and thereafter she herself. This rite performed, the Bishop pronounced the marriage blessing and without further marriage play – the buffooning, the lewd jest – for already the groom looked weary to death, the whole company, saluting towards the bed, stepped backwards leaving those two alone.

She lay as they had placed her, facing the groom, and did not move. He stretched out a lean arm to press her close. She felt his body hard through the bone where it should be padded with the muscles of a man's strength, felt it soft and drooping in that man's member where it should have been hard and erect. For all she was a virgin she knew the strength of a man when his passion is roused. Charles Brandon had held her in a last farewell, and through the thickness of her gown she had felt him alive with passion, and with like passion had responded. And now, nothing; nothing but this travesty of a man; a man that should be dandling his grandchildren, trying to take to himself a woman young enough to be one of them.

For the moment she was overcome with disgust. Then she saw a tear gather in his eye, fall slow upon the withered cheek . . . and pitied him. He had wed from desire to get him a son; and also because he had been fired by a lust too great for his feeble body. Now his eye pleaded what his tongue could not utter; nor her own tongue, to save his pride, express. She put her hand between those impotent thighs and, without words, gave him her promise. From her no soul should know his secret. He laid his head upon her breast and she let it lie, their roles reversed. She was the mother to comfort him, her child. And in that moment a tenderness in her, that was not love nor ever could be, was born. Presently he sighed, turned over in the bed and like a child was suddenly asleep. He slept lightly as the old do; and presently, missing the known comfort of his own bed, stumbled from his place and struck upon the bell; then, escorted by two gentlemen of the Bedchamber, he left her to herself.

And now she could no longer endure the bed that smelled of old age; she called very low for Lady Guildford who came at once. My lady covered her child's nakedness with a bedgown and led her into the closet. It was fresh there and cold; my lady blew upon the braziers, put on more coal, and settled the Queen in the great chair. She brought her mistress wine and the girl drank thirstily, surprised to find her throat parched.

She lay back in the great chair and said nothing; there was no need . . . no need to discuss the pitiful secret that was no secret. For a while there was silence; then the Queen, trying to free her mind from the pitiful, distressful scene in the bedroom, asked about the young girl that had walked interlaced with Anne Bullen, sharing that secret and smothered laughter.

'She is no virgin, that one, for all her few years. Soon she is to be married and pray God her husband take her from the court and keep her in some virtue – real or pretended. He is Monsieur de Brézé, Grand Seneschal of Normandy; at present she is Mademoiselle Diane de Poitiers. If she be pregnant – as I think – who shall say whether the child she carries be her husband's or her lover's? And that lover? All Paris and beyond knows well: Duke Francis, that some call the Dauphin. The King's heir he is, but Dauphin he is not nor ever can be. None may bear that title save the King's own son!'

But for all that Duke Francis will be King . . .

Their eyes met, each woman assuring the other.

'They say there's no faithfulness in her, that she was born to be men's mistress. But that's not true. She was born to be a King's mistress – and to that ambition she will be faithful. She has a robust young vigour that takes men's fancies. There are, you may guess, tales and to spare of her! They say the old King, before your match was made, himself would have her in his bed but . . .'

'Why trouble the Queen with such vile tales?' Diane de Poitiers stood in the doorway. She was full-dressed, dark eyes aflame with fury.

'We have not summoned you, Mademoiselle,' the Queen said. 'Still less given you permission to enter! Do you, perhaps, play spy? And who pays you for the part?'

Diane de Poitiers curtseyed very low, but anger lit her cheeks and throbbed in her pulses. So afire she was with life the Queen felt a pale thing beside her. No wonder this de Poitiers drew the men like moths to a flame.

'Madam Queen,' she said, and could scarce speak for the hard beat of the pulse in that round white throat of hers, 'I am no spy!'

'Then what do you here in the Queen's closet?' Lady Guildford asked.

'I come to protect her,' she said, bold and daring, 'and to protect myself from the lies that go about concerning me, in which you, my lady Guildford, have this night played your part; and for that part you shall pay!' She turned her back on my lady and addressed herself to the Queen. 'I would not have the Queen who is so new to our court distressed, no, nor misled, neither.'

'The tales are lies then?'

'That the King wanted me for his mistress! The Queen may judge of that lie for herself!' And her fine eyes were spiteful.

'And you are no man's mistress?'

'I am betrothed, Madam, and soon to be wed!'

'You have not answered me!'

'My answer is *no*!' She stared down the Queen with great bold eyes that did not waver for all her lying.

'Well, Mademoiselle, you have done your *devoir*. You have warned me. Now you may go!'

Diane de Poitiers curtseyed very low; she walked backwards to the very door and her excessive courtesy was a mockery. She shut the door gently and so was gone.

'We have made an enemy there!' the Queen said.

'You are the Queen and need have no fear,' Lady Guildford said. 'But I!'

'If she hurts you she hurts me. I will protect you.'

Chapter Twenty

She had scarce closed her eyes in sleep when there came a knocking at her door. It was not my lady Guildford, as she had expected, but the Bullen girl whom she had certainly not expected; upon a small velvet cushion she carried a morning gift from the groom. It was a great ruby, hung upon a double chain to take its weight. There seemed no end to the old man's desire to pleasure his young bride.

She must rise at once to thank the King; but even as the young woman reached for the Queen's bedgown it struck Mary once again that Lady Guildford should be with her now, not this Anne Bullen whom she did not like. Had the sleepless night watching over the Queen tired my lady? Was she otherwise indisposed? Mistress Anne, questioned, casting down her eyes, said she did not know, and Mary must put by the question until, fit to receive the King's gentleman, the great ruby a wound upon her white throat, she had expressed humble and grateful thanks for so magnificent a gift. Duty done, she proceeded to inquire for her guardian angel, her second mother, Lady Guildford.

There they stood, her young ladies, surprise and consternation upon all their faces; all save one. Mistress Anne, very demure, said, 'My lady Guildford is packing her baggage.' And while the Queen sought for words to express disbelief in so ridiculous a statement, Mistress Anne added, 'She has her orders to return home!'

'Mistress, you know not what you say!' In her relief Mary all but laughed in the girl's face. It was unthinkable that the kind old man that sought in every way to pleasure his wife should deprive her of one who had been a mother to her – Lady Guildford who had been her childhood's guide and should guide her in any difficulty in this new life. But presently in came my lady herself, dressed for travel, her comely face all stained with tears; never before had Mary seen her wise mentor weep; and now, indeed, she began to fear the incredible truth.

'What shall I do without you? It is very clear I cannot! The King desires nothing but my happiness. Without you I cannot be content in this strange court and so I shall tell him!'

'That last you must not say. It will give great offence.'

'Then I must urge my need of your wise counsel.'

'He will tell you there are others to instruct you. Madam, you may spare yourself the trouble.'

But for all that she would not be gainsaid; and the King, having signified his pleasure to receive her, she went, shaken but still not quite convinced, to his bedchamber. He was sitting up in bed, bedgown thrown upon his withered nakedness, and after kneeling to kiss his hand and receiving his salute upon her mouth, she came to her point at once; and immediately received his answer: 'I would – as I think I have shown – do all for the Queen's happiness. But that happiness I consider to be endangered by Lady Guildford.'

'How so, sir?' And though she was humble in her asking, his brow darkened. He was all unused to being questioned.

'Because, Madam, the lady is a stumbling-block between my wife and me. From the moment you set foot here in France you have not been seen save she stood by you, directing you this way and that. You must not speak to any, not even to myself, your husband and your King, save she stood by to hear every word. The wonder is, Madam, she did not make a third in the marriage-bed!'

She might well have done for all the good you got from that! The thought leaped instant to her mind.

'But, Madam, I make no doubt she was there, all ears, in the next room.'

He was so near the truth there was no answer to that. And

159

he went on, 'Let me remind you, Madam, you are Queen of France and no infant to be directed this way and that by an old nurse!'

'Sir,' she said, very humble, 'the Lady Guildford is no nurse but my second mother. My brother himself entreated her to accompany me into France, though she had rather retire into the country.'

'Then she shall have her wish!' and his smile laid bare his toothless gums.

She might not know all the intricacies of the French court; but she knew enough to know that one does not argue with the King of France. Her own anger was such that she could have torn the ruby from her throat and flung it in his face. She made her curtsey and departed.

A mischief-maker, a gossiping tongue! The de Poitiers of course. *We have made an enemy there!* She herself had said it, last night; and she had been right, right.

Back in her closet she sent for my lord of Norfolk. He came at once, all smiling courtesy; and she, having swallowed her anger before the King, now let fly.

'My lord, you have served me ill. You know the love I bear my lady Guildford. For myself I can stand humiliation; I can deal with it – though I do not relish it. For I am, after all, the Queen and who dare laugh in my face. But my lady Guildford? That's another matter!'

'Madam, be comforted. The Lady Guildford is not the only one to return home. There go with her a great company of ladies and gentlemen. Here, Madam, is the list.'

'You had best,' she told him, 'read the names of those that remain.'

'Dorset's two sisters and his daughter – your kinswomen, all three; and Mistress Anne Bullen.' He stopped. She waited. And when he said no more. . .

'Four ladies, only. . .' she interrupted, not believing her ears. 'What attendance is that for the Queen of France?'

'The King has chosen others.'

'The de Poitiers, no doubt.'

'Duke Francis asked it. But if Madam the Queen objects . . .'

'I do object. I'll not have her, the Duke's mistress, spying upon me. She has worked me enough mischief already.'

'Madam the Queen would be wise to win her as a friend!' And was this a warning or a threat?

'I choose my own friends. Now, as to Mistress Bullen – I do not want her about my person.'

'Has she offended the Queen?' She felt the hard base of stone beneath his smiling.

She was forced to admit there had been no offence.

'Then, Madam, would you disgrace so young a girl on the threshold of her life – and no reason? Madam, it does not become a Queen. As to Mistress Bullen, she shall serve you in proper fashion; my head shall answer it. Now, Madam, as to your chamberwomen . . .'

She was forced to let the matter of his niece drop. He was, after all, right; the girl had committed no offence.

'Madam the Queen, I hope . . .'

'I'll thank you, my lord, to keep your hopes to yourself. You have not served me well.'

'I am sorry you should think it, Madam; yet I am confident that in time – and no great time neither – you shall change your mind. Young ladies, though they be Queens, are not always wise judges of what shall serve them best. One last word, Madam . . .'

'My lord, I am weary of your advice. I wish you *bon voyage*, back to England. And by God' – she burst out – 'I would I might return thither.' She turned her back, impatient; the inclined head, the swept bonnet went unseen.

What now? To appeal once more to the old man who sought her happiness yet took from her her only comfort was useless. Her brother? She must write to him at once; Lady Guildford should take the letter. But there were things best left unwritten – the name of the de Poitiers girl, for instance. My lady should round out the picture, should tell him all.

She began with her salutations, her surprise that she had not heard from him since she left home; and so came to the heart of the matter.

. . . I am left suddenly alone. For, on the next morning after my marriage, my chamberlain and all my other men servants were discharged. And, in like wise, my mother Guildford with my other women and maidens, except those that never had experience nor knowledge how to warn me or give me counsel in time of need; which is to be feared more shortly than your Grace though at the time of my departing, as my mother Guildford can more plainly show your Grace than I can write; to whom I beseech you to give credence.

If it be by any means possible, I humbly require you to cause my said mother Guildford to repair hither once again. For, if any chance happen other than well, I shall not know where nor of whom to seek any good counsel that shall be to your pleasure nor yet my own profit. I marvel much that my lord of Norfolk should at all times grant everything at their request here.

I am well assured that when you know the truth of everything as my mother Guildford can show you, you would little have thought that I should have been thus entreated. Would to God my lord Archbishop of York had come with me in place of Norfolk, for then I am sure I should have been left much more to my heart's content than I am now.

And thus I bid your Grace Farewell and more heart's ease than I have now.

From Abbeville, this XII day of October.

Give greetings to my mother Guildford.

By the hand of your loving sister,

Mary Queen of France

But still she was disturbed. Her brother's vanity would certainly be pricked; yet in the press of affairs – business or pleasure – he might let it pass. She must write to him that ruled the King, to Wolsey, her friend, how they had unceremoniously packed home my lady Guildford.

. . . . by whom, as you know, the King and you willed me in every wise to be counselled.

My lord, as you love the King my brother and me, find means that she, in all haste, may be sent to me again, for I would as lief lose the winnings I shall have in France as to lose her counsel. I pray, my lord, give credence to my mother Guildford concerning this matter.

She laid down her pen; then, remembering the enmity between Wolsey and Norfolk, added:

Since my lord of Norfolk has neither dealt his best for me nor yet for her, I pray you always to be a good lord to her.

And would to God fortune been so good as to have had you with me here, instead of my lord of Norfolk.

My lord, I pray you give credence to the tale of my sorrows which she shall deliver unto you.

This XII day of October

Yours, while I live,

Mary

To my loving friend the Archbishop of York.

Chapter Twenty-one

Now she sat alone in her desolate rooms. Somewhere she could hear laughter and knew it for that of Anne Bullen and the de Poitiers. Queen of France she might be; but the most wretched woman in Christendom she certainly was! Her tears fell fast; she thought, *For every jewel I have paid and shall pay not with a kiss but with a tear.* And wept again for very loneliness.

She started at the opening of the door. Who dared intrude unasked upon the Queen of France? There could be but one. His heart misgiving, though his wits applauding, this cutting-off of useless wood, the King himself had come to comfort her.

She rose to her curtsey.

'Madam,' he said, 'here is something shall dry all tears.' The old shaking hand held out a jewel that sparkled brighter than any tear. It was a great square-cut diamond of purest water, set upon a chain of gold, and beneath it a pearl of equal size, of perfect shape and colour. 'It is my best jewel!' And there was a simplicity about him that softened her heart. 'Duke Francis would give all he possesses for this! It is called the "Mirror of Naples". The most beautiful jewel in Christendom for the most beautiful lady in Christendom.'

The old, trembling hands fastened it about her neck; and though she would have given back the jewel – for all that jewels were a passion with her – in return for Lady Guildford, she kissed the grey cheek, hoping without hope that she might have both – jewel and lady.

Now, her tears dried, though her heart wept still, the great jewel shining upon her bosom, he besought her to leave her closet to shine once more upon the court. And, since weeping neither became her nor helped her – for in the matter of Lady Guildford he was adamant, being jealous of her influence and the love his Queen bore the woman – she lifted a smiling face, curtseyed her assent and went with him. But for all that she grieved; and feared too, lest she make some false step. That same day the King pressed upon her more jewels, rings and bracelets, coronets and girdles, brooches and buckles, more than any woman could wear in a lifetime. And for each she must pay with a kiss. A foolish and distasteful procedure, she thought. But she was not a Tudor for nothing; not only did she love a fine jewel for its own sake, she knew besides its usefulness at need. The King was a sick man; sometimes when she looked upon him, when he slept upon a day-bed, she thought, *He is dead . . . who shall protect me in this strange land?* And knew her answer. *Duke Francis; but at a price. Not even the Miroir de Naples would suffice. . . .*

Beneath her gracious smiling she waited sick at heart for a reply from Wolsey or from her brother. Surely her one small request would be granted. That my lord of Worcester, the English Ambassador, had sought audience with the King of France and had written Wolsey his somewhat biased account of it, taking it upon himself to declare all troubles smoothed, she was not to know. According to Worcester, he had himself gone to ask for the return of Lady Guildford, but the King had cried out with an old man's petulance, 'My wife and I agree perfectly in this matter. We are both of age; we do not look to have servants to rule her or me.' And when my lord, according to himself, would have pressed still further, the King had cut him short. 'If my wife has need of counsel, then I am able to give it.'

After a brooding silence, suddenly he had struck his old hand upon his chair's arm until Worcester, so he said, thought the bones would crack, and had cried out vehement as a child, 'I will not, I tell you, have that woman about my wife! I am not well. . . . When I am able to make merry with my wife, I do not care for strange women about me.'

When I am able to make merry with my wife. . . . . And what, wondered Wolsey, studying the letter, had the old man meant by that? By making merry did he mean playing his husband's part? And had my Lady Guildford guessed at his impotence? Whatever was unclear in Worcester's letter, one thing was clear enough. The French King would have no more of my lady.

So when, at last, her answer from England did come, it was not at all what Mary had looked for. Wolsey wrote that it was King Henry's sovereign will and pleasure that she should content herself without my lady Guildford and continue to put a pleasant face upon the matter.

Having given her time to swallow her grievous news, Worcester sent to beg an audience.

'Madam,' he said, 'I trust you are now content in the matter?'

She answered him with another question. 'And my lady? What recompense – if recompense there can be – for her most undeserved humiliation?'

'A pension, Madam; twenty pounds a year.'

Twenty pounds a year! For all those years of loving service a miserable twenty pounds! She knew her brother would never be over-generous in matters that made no show; but this! She had not counted upon such a piece of meanness.

A smiling face may cover a sore heart, but smiles beget smiles in others; the Queen's pleasant ways begot kindness in others. She was fêted, poems were written in her honour, she was loaded with gifts. The King doted upon her – and the court must follow – or appear to follow his example. She could, it appeared, do no wrong. A smiling heart began to match a smiling face. The old man, for all his obstinacy, had not been wrong in thinking her happier freed from the tutelage of her old governess. Without my lady constantly in attendance, advising this or that, the Queen took on the full dignity of her station. In her household she had her four English ladies and her two English chamberers; she still could not like Anne Bullen but the girl behaved well enough – no doubt her uncle Norfolk had warned her. And, in addition, the King had chosen the best ladies in France for her service, and he had, too, had the grace to remove the de Poitiers girl.

And there were royal ladies at court only too glad to befriend the young Queen. Mary found she could do very well without Lady Guildford; that she was, after all, Queen of France and could do as she pleased – which was true enough, so long as she did her duty to please the King. Fond and foolish he might be, but he was still . . . the King.

King Louis was, but a man far from well. In the early days of his marriage, he tried to play the gallant groom, and almost killed himself in the process. To please his young wife he stayed up later than his habit, he rested less during the day, he exerted himself in the festivities, and soon both were paying the price. Mary found herself less bride than nurse, and was content it should be so. Her vigorous young body shrank from contact with his; but her natural kindliness made it easy to return kindness for kindness. She looked to his comfort and his dignity. She would persuade him to bed at his former hour; he would come into her bedchamber at six o'clock every night, and into her bed. She, in a bedgown, would sit upon a stool by his side, talking to the gaunt figure beneath the blue velvet coverlet stitched with roses red and white; or she would sing to him very softly and he would fall into a light sleep; and on his awaking she would call for his confidential valet to help the old man into his bedroom and take him away. It was a ritual they went through every night. That he slept in the Queen's bed satisfied his honour.

After that first night he had tried once or twice to get the Queen with child; but soon he gave up the useless effort. He was content, for very weakness, to sit up in the bed and look about the pretty room, with the chair of gold and purple in which she sat, with its hangings of cloth-of-gold, its fine statues and ornaments. 'Pretty,' he would say. 'Pretty things for a pretty lady.' He would say it half a dozen times within the same hour, forgetting that he had said it but a little while since.

Then, when he was back in the safety of his own room, she would dress again and steal away to find what amusement she might, and amusement there was in plenty. She might dance, sing, join the card-players; or flirt, if she chose. But that last she never did choose – though there was opportunity enough. She cherished the dignity of the old man, her husband. As for Brandon, of him she seldom thought; in this new life he had become far away as a dream.

Brandon might be far away as a dream but not Catherine, her brother's wife, her own dear friend, and Catherine's time was drawing near. Mary prayed for her sister-in-law night and morning; lighting candles, making offerings that Catherine be safe delivered – of a son if God would be so gloriously merciful; if not, a daughter: a daughter would be mercy enough! She had given orders that news of Catherine be brought to her at once, even though she should be in the midst of her crowning.

Now the King was somewhat rested, all was ready for their progress to Paris for the Queen's coronation. About to ride forth, a last-minute attack of gout forced the King back to his couch. 'I am weary to death of Abbeville!' Mary cried out petulant, and was immediately ashamed, for the King bore his pain with cheerfulness, nor would he allow her to forgo any pleasure.

'I love to see you happy. It makes me well again,' he would say; and he would sit, his eyes following her and nothing but these eyes showing his body's pain.

Chapter Twenty-two

At long last they were able to leave Abbeville; towards the end of October they rode in high procession to Beauvais. Weary Mary might be of Abbeville, but the nearer they approached Beauvais, the sicker grew her heart with apprehension, yet stabbed with a most fearful joy. For at Beauvais she must see Brandon again; she could not escape it. Duke Francis had arranged a great joust in honour of the marriage, open to all comers from any country in Christendom. England had sent two challengers to prove themselves for England's honours. And those two? Dorset, her kinsman . . . and Suffolk.

Brandon was, after all, England's finest knight. Yet she could not but wonder that her brother had risked sending him. But then Henry had not known – or if knowing had not seriously believed – that she was so deeply in love; and certainly he would rely upon her sense of propriety not to cause gossip in the courts of Christendom. She wondered whether the old man, her husband, knew of her love for Brandon and whether he were jealous. Yet, whatever he knew, whatever he felt, the King of France must greet both visitors with equal courtesy, since both had been named ambassadors extraordinary.

Arrived at his lodgings in Beauvais, Charles Brandon was asking himself these same questions. He had had his own doubts of the wisdom of sending him to the French court. But he had very much wanted to go; after a wedding and before a crowning, the court would be gay indeed. He was curious, besides, to set eyes on his love; or, to put it more accurately, his lover. Married she might be, but he could not seriously believe she felt either affection or duty for her old husband – while he, himself, had taken two or three ladies to his bed since their parting.

Now, standing in his favourite spot in any chamber – before the looking-glass – he saw himself a fine enough man to turn any lady's head even a Queen's . . . and he was a free man. His wife Anne was dead and the wife of his annulled marriage had wed again. The girl that was now Queen of France was – or would have been – just the one for him. Mary was beautiful, she was clever, she was gentle, amiable and gay . . . and she had loved him with all her heart. He had seen no woman to equal her. But if as Princess she had been beyond his reach, how much more now that she was Queen of France!

He was still admiring himself, twirling his cloak this way and that, when the Sieur de Clermont was announced; he had come to bid both gentlemen welcome and to desire my lord of Suffolk to wait upon the King as soon as might be, and alone.

Brandon refreshed himself with food, changed his travelling clothes, set a jewel in his bonnet and, humming a little, made his way to the royal presence. At this last moment he had some renewed misgivings. *Had* the old man heard . . . anything? The French Ambassador at home was all eyes and ears. Why must Suffolk come at once and *alone*? He reassured himself. A courtesy, an especial courtesy, not merely to an ambassador but to the King of England's friend.

Brandon resumed his humming.

Mary sat in her usual place by the King's bed. She did not expect to see Brandon today, for the King was too sick to rise. But her mind could not, in all her efforts, turn from him she so longed and feared to see. How would it be with her when she set eyes upon the man she so passionately loved? How, looking upon that healthy, handsome body, could she turn again in pity and loyalty to her old, sick husband? Must not her pity be for herself, her loyalty to her own young, clamouring body? Now she prayed God she might never see her love again; now she prayed, desperate, that he come soon, soon; rejoice her dreary days with the sight of him.

Beneath her quiet face the battle raged; the battle she had believed won.

She was aroused from her thoughts by the shock of hearing his name as the page announced him. In he came, bonnet sweeping the ground, handsomer even than she remembered, or any man had the right to be. To believe him of the same species, even if twenty years or more younger than the old man in the bed, was not possible. He bowed deep to the Queen and then kneeled by the bedside. The King stretched out a withered arm, dry and thin as a stick. 'My lord of Suffolk,' he said in his quavering old voice, 'you are most heartily welcome.'

'Sir,' Brandon replied, kneeling still, 'I hope I see you in good health.'

'Resting . . . resting . . . for the festivities to come. I trust you shall not put our own champions to shame!' And then, 'Madam the Queen is, I believe, an old friend of yours.'

Brandon rose from his knees and went to kneel to the Queen. Had she ever been mad enough to think she had forgotten him? The touch of his lips upon her flesh sent the wild blood racing in her veins. But still her face showed nothing but courteous welcome; from infancy she had been well disciplined in courtly behaviour.

'I trust my brother of England is well,' the old man said. 'I am bound to love him best of all men in Christendom since he has given me my greatest treasure . . . my wife.'

'There is, sir, no man more fit to win such a treasure. God grant that you may enjoy her for many years to come. It is my King's wish and' – he kept his voice steady – 'my own.' But the light heart within him pitied so much youth and beauty sacrificed to an old decaying man; and an old man who could take no fleshly pleasure in the sacrifice.

'Tell my good brother of England that I am his servant, to serve him in any way at his pleasure. We are brothers now, not only in kinship but in arms.'

'Sir, you take time by the forelock. That same message I was commissioned to deliver to you.'

'Then, my lord, he and I are in accord.'

So, compliments being exchanged, the Ambassador took his leave. 'My lord,' the old man said, 'there are messages, no doubt, your master sends to his sister, the Queen; and there are questions she will, no doubt, wish to ask. She shall send for you at her good will.'

Mary bowed her head. Never would she allow Brandon into her closet, no, nor into any place where they might hold private conversation. Seeing him again she dared not trust herself with him, and they two alone.

Moved, in spite of himself, by the Queen's young beauty that once he had held in his arms, touched by her sweet bearing to the old man, knowing her deep love for himself, Brandon felt his own light heart stir in response. He thrust away his madness; somewhat disconsolate he sat himself down to write to his King.

. . . I assure your Grace there was never Queen of France that carried herself more honourably, nor wiselier . . . And, as for the King, there was never man that set his mind more upon a woman than he does upon her, which I am sure will be no little comfort to your Grace. It rejoiced me not a little – your Grace knows why.

Henry frowned over the last words. Of course he knew why. So young a woman, the sap rising full and quick; so old a man, the sap withered and dry. Yet still a tree that, like some oaks, three-quarters dead, live on. . . . Tactless of Brandon to have made that point. Yet, if the King of France were such an oak, how long would her honour and her wisdom last? How long could they last?

He must write such a letter that, while praising her, warned her as to her future conduct. Yet it must be done discreetly so that she alone caught the note of warning. In the end it was not to his sister that he wrote, nor yet to his friend, but to her husband:

> . . . we have heard how she conducts herself towards you in all humility and reverence so that you are well-content with her; and we have conceived very great joy, pleasure and comfort in hearing this. And our will and intention is, that, so acting, she should persevere from good to better, if she wish to have our brotherly benevolence. We make no doubt that you will, day by day, find her more and more all she ought to be, and that she shall do everything that shall be to your will, pleasure and contentment . . .

Henry was right in supposing she would take this to be both warning and advice. She needed none. She had already determined upon her conduct. Yet to keep Brandon at a distance was not easy. Seeing her so desirable and so desired – for Duke Francis made no secret of his passion – Brandon, never a discreet man, took every opportunity to waylay her. Once, coming across her as she stood in the embrasure of a window, he whispered, 'We waste our time. The old man will never be well; and it's the creaking gate that lasts the longest.'

'So long as the creaking gate lasts, I am content,' she said. But they knew, both of them, that she belied her own heart.

The procession went its slow way to Paris, the King within the litter, she riding gallant beside him that the people might see her. Even so it was overmuch for him. More than once she begged him to stop and rest. 'The tourneys can wait a little,' she told him.

'But not the crowning of my Queen. With my own eyes I must see it. My son must be born of a crowned Queen.'

She said nothing to that. He was so confused at times; did he think that on their wedding-night and on the nights that had followed, before he fell asleep in her arms, he had made such approach that she might conceive? She did not undeceive him. Let him keep his pride as a man. It could make no difference to the succession.

Fifth day of November, day of her crowning; a day shrouded in mist that soon cleared to show as fair a day as one could hope for a winter crowning.

It was scarce daylight when in came her women to dress her; and glad she was of the French chamberers who knew their duty well. When she was ready there came her ladies, all with open-hearted admiration, save that in the eyes of the Bullen girl there was clear envy. And there came also, not in duty alone but out of free-hearted kindness, the Princess Claude.

The distance between the royal lodgings and the cathedral was short, which was a pity; for such a procession is seen but once in a lifetime. First the princes of the Church, then the peers, walking each with his lady, and the high officers of State, each one magnificent in his great robes. Thereafter, immediately before the Queen, came the Princes of the Blood with, upon a cushion, the regalia. And now came she for whom all eyes waited – the Queen herself, walking beneath a canopy of Estate, Duke Francis holding her by the hand. So beautiful she was that, as she passed, there came from the crowds a long-drawn sigh of pleasure awaited and satisfied. Her golden hair flowed free, her gown of gold tissue, stitched with *fleurs-de-lys* in pearls and cut low in the French fashion, showed to perfection the white neck and bosom and the beautiful face. The great mantle of purple velvet, edged and lined with ermine, was carried by her four English ladies dressed alike in gowns of silver with sashes of Tudor green. Behind them walked the ambassadors, other princes and distinguished guests come to honour this day.

The King himself was not present. He wished, he said, his Queen to shine alone in her glory; but indeed he felt himself too weak for so high, so moving a ceremony.

The procession entered the cathedral doors, to be welcomed

by the supreme princes of the Church – the archbishops and cardinals. Then Duke Francis led the Queen, followed by her ladies, to an anteroom, there to wait until all were seated. What, she wondered, did he make of today's crowning? Did he wonder whether she carried within her the seed that should be the next King? She did not know, nor had she any intention of easing his mind on that score. She could not but be charmed by him – she was a woman – but she did not trust him. He had more than once uttered words in her ear too flattering to be true; and if true, entirely improper. He had pressed her hand far too close, and his kisses were not always the formal salute they should be.

Now, when every prince of State and Church was in his allotted place – the English ambassadors in the high seats of honour – the trumpets rang out; and at their notes she rose and, with her ladies bearing up her train and Duke Francis taking her once more by the hand, came into the church.

In the great doorway stood the Princes of the Blood, each bearing his cushion with the regalia. Duke Francis, still holding her by the hand, led her to the high altar. Passing, she caught sight of Brandon sitting at the end of the choir to the right of her; so near, so near she could have touched his sleeve. At this moment in the midst of all the pageantry, she longed for the touch of him; yet, at the same time, she felt a great pride in being crowned.

Before the high altar, her ladies arranging her train and Duke Francis still holding her hand, she knelt upon a cushion and silently prayed. Then, the Cardinal de Brie who had conducted her marriage service, anointed her, still kneeling, with the holy oils. And, upon her rising, he placed the sceptre in her right hand, the rod of justice in her left, upon her marriage finger the ring that should wed her to this people, and upon her golden flowing hair the crown of the Queen of France. To the jubilant cries of 'God save the Queen', three times ringing to the high roof of the church, her hand once more within that of the Duke and her ladies bearing up her train, she went with slow care and a beautiful carriage to the throne beneath the canopy of Estate on the left side of the altar.

It was but a few steps yet already she felt the weight of the metal upon her head; her neck could scarce bear the strain. Panic took her. *If I cannot support this weight, what shall I do? My neck is breaking beneath the burden of the crown.*

She had forgotten that Duke Francis had been appointed to help her in this matter. Seated, she felt the weight lifted and knew that he stood behind her great chair and with both hands held the crown a little above her head. And now, High Mass having been sung, she must once more make the few steps to the altar to present her offering and to receive the sacrament.

And, the great congregation standing, she passed from the church back to the Queen's lodgings to rest; and again the people cried out their love and admiration, but now it was to all-but-deaf ears. She was weary with the ceremony, yet she was withal exalted. She was Queen of France. That evening, in the Presence Chamber, she received the congratulations of the ambassadors; but, as was proper because they were her countrymen and new-come into France, my lord of Dorset and my lord of Suffolk were received in private audience.

The correct things had been said and graciously acknowledged and the two ambassadors were about to depart when Brandon said, 'Madam, I bear your Grace private greetings from my master the King and from Madam Catherine, his wife.' So, Dorset having bowed himself away, Brandon seized his chance.

'Madam,' he said very low, 'when I saw Valois take you by the hand, when I saw him stand there behind you, to save you from the weight of the crown, I all but ran mad with jealousy.'

'It is not your privilege, my lord, to carry a weight for me.' Her heart beat hard in her breast, yet her voice was indifferent.

'Yet carry a weight for your sake I do, and must. Here!' And he laid his hand upon his heart.

'That's a weight you have no right to carry. I am married. You, yourself, have written home of my happiness!'

'Happiness!' He let his palms fall downwards, empty. 'You – and with *him*!'

'It is a happiness that maybe you do not choose to see.' But for all that her voice trembled.

'Happiness!' he cried out again. 'Madam, I feel no jealousy, only pity for one that, having so great a treasure, cannot enjoy it.'

'Your compliment goes beyond courtesy. Let us make an end of such talk. You are to speak to me of my brother and of Madam Queen Catherine. Is she well? And God send that the old, sad pattern of her childbearing be broken.'

'Madam Queen Catherine is near her time and well enough. But who can tell?' He shrugged a little. 'God send her safe delivery and England the hope of its heir. Madam, we pray for it!'

'Amen!' She rose and walked restless about the room. 'Tell my sister I pray for her day and night. My lord, farewell.'

'Am I not to see you again?' And his lips lingered overlong upon her hand.

'You are to fight in the tourneys, are you not?' And she withdrew her hand. 'I wish you good fortune for your honour and that of my country.'

'There can be no good fortune for me any more in this world,' he told her. She knew his nature to be changeable, but in this moment she could not doubt his misery.

Her breath came forth in a sigh, as it were in spite of herself. 'My lord, we neither of us can change our lot. This is farewell.'

Chapter Twenty-three

They were for Paris next day. When she awoke Mary found the King already gone; he had driven off early to assure himself that all was prepared to receive the Queen. At nine of the clock, the Queen herself left in high procession, and halted at the Chapelle St Denis hard by the walls of Paris. There, having dined, she awaited the procession from the city that was to join her own before she entered in state.

The November sky had long darkened to deep night before the magnificent train turned towards the St Pol Palace – home she could not call it. But even now there was no rest. She must be gowned afresh in yet another golden dress for the State banquet at the Palais de Justice.

As she came in at the door the King rose and the whole company with him. She came to the great chair and kneeling before him offered her gift – a tiny shield of gold bearing the cross of St George. Wolsey had sent it with instructions that she herself, and none other, must give it into the King's hand – wordless pledge of peace between their two countries.

The lovely girl, aglitter from head to foot, kneeling to the old sick man, was a sight to make the company take in its breath with wonder and some pity. The King, gracious, accepted the gift, kissed the giver upon both cheeks, held out a hand that she might rise, and led her to her place.

A long feast, interminable; but she had for all her weariness the appetite of youth, and the good food and wine restored her. She listened with pleasure to the excellent music; she danced with less pleasure, for she must be led out upon the floor by Duke Francis who never ceased his whisperings. . . . 'The people are mad for you; they say you are beautiful as an angel. But there was never an angel so beautiful; angels wear the grace of angels only, but the Queen wears the grace of the Queen of Heaven.'

Mary received this as a courtier's speech and rewarded him with a smile; but when he whispered that the crowds were saying – and not softly either – that it was himself she should have married and not the old man, she, remembering his wife's gentleness and the kindliness of her, showed not so much as by a flicker of the eyelids that she had heard the words. This Duke, they said, so debonair, could catch any woman in the world with his charm – but not herself. Her word was pledged and her hand given. And her heart too was given and could never be her own again.

No need to go out again into the cold night: bedchambers stood ready within the Palais de Justice. And, the King retiring early, she went with him, he to his chamber and she to hers. This night he made no pretence to come to her and it was wonderful to be alone. She stood in her furred bedgown and looked down upon sleeping Paris for the first time. Dark the winter sky; darker still the towers and spires patterned thereon. And now, the moon riding high, she could see the Seine shining like a tinsel riband; and she thought of England and the dear familiar Thames that runs by Westminster, by Greenwich and Richmond, and she longed with a deep passionate yearning to be home again.

She slept late into the morning; waking and coming to her closet, she paused at the half-open door. Her ladies were already assembled, and above the murmur of voices one voice rose clear – that of Anne Bullen. 'Madam the Queen retires early and sleeps late. Well, that is to be looked for in a bride!' She spoke with an unashamed lewdness that mocked bride and groom. 'Well, but such a groom! I doubt it is worth sleeping with an old man even if it make you a Queen!'

'A Queen, mistress, you will never be!' Mary came into the room. 'You may make your mind easy on that score. Mistress, you may go!'

179

Green beneath her sallow skin, the girl rose, and with the others she went down upon her curtsey; and then curtseyed herself out of the room.

The Queen rode back to St Pol, dined and changed her gown to ride once more through Paris to the Tournelles Palace where the King lodged. She drove through the great porch to the noise of hammering and the sight of workmen busy erecting seats in readiness for the great tournament in which Charles Brandon, Duke of Suffolk, and my lord the Earl of Dorset were to joust for England's honour.

That night, after supper, the King retired at his usual hour of six o'clock. If he retired, so must the Queen, should he desire to keep up the honourable show of virility. Her women had removed her gown of State and put upon her her bed-gown; they had taken off the caul and tied back her hair with a riband when a knock fell upon her door. A page in Suffolk's livery prayed entry for his lord. In the next room her women were busy about the bed, turning down the sheets, putting wine upon the table, blowing upon the embers. For these few moments she was alone. That she should refuse him entry she knew well; but the thing was beyond her. See him she must, if only to forbid him in future.

In he came, so handsome that her heart leaped, yet so pale, so melancholy that it dropped again. And he, seeing her so, without the attributes of queenship, seeing her as he had never seen her before – a woman in her bedgown – was fired suddenly, unexpectedly to passion.

'Madam,' he went down upon both knees, his face desperate, 'I am come to bid the Queen goodbye. I am for England on the next tide!'

'You cannot go!' Her face was white now, as desperate as his own. 'You are named in the lists.'

'I cannot stay. Nor can I acquit myself with honour thinking of you fondled by the old man!' And, sounds coming from the bedchamber beyond, he added, 'Aye, and bedded, too.'

To that she made no answer. Love Brandon she did, but

honour and gratitude forbade mention of the King's impotence.

'Then you should never have come,' she said very quiet. 'Certain it is you cannot go. To go is to overthrow the order of the lists. And more, it is insult to the King of France, and to the King your master. Your friend he may be, but for all that he will not forgive you!'

'A true knight fights for his lady – to wear her favour and to bring her honour.'

'What honour to a woman already wed? As for me I need no further honour. I am Queen of France!'

'Without my lady's favour I cannot fight.'

'Then choose your lady.'

'I have chosen.'

'My lord,' she said, 'wear what favour you will upon your arm; this you may wear upon your heart.' She plucked the riband that held her hair for the night. He put it to his lips, thrust it within his doublet and was gone.

Back came the women, laughing and chattering that all was prepared; and again came her husband to play the usual farce.

Chapter Twenty-four

You may seal a peace with marriage, but when enmity lies beneath how long shall such a peace last? Between England and France enmity had been long and bitter; the great tourney showed it only too clearly.

In the park of the Tournelles Palace on Tuesday the twenty-first of November all was ready; the ground measured and railed off, a high platform for the royal party, seats erected behind the barriers for the good burghers of Paris, while lesser folk stood or climbed where they might – prentice lads sat like birds in every tree. At the entrance to the lists upon a triumphal arch supported by five pillars, five shields were displayed; each shield signified combat with an especial weapon – lance, spear, sword and javelin, or with two weapons. Each challenger, if he wished to enter for an especial combat, touched the particular shield with the point of his lance and hung his own shield beneath it; below these hung the shields of those that had accepted the challenge. High above all, upon the arch itself, stood the shields of England and France.

The King, unable to sit up long, lay upon a raised couch; by his side sat Mary, behind her the Princess Claude and the high peeresses of France, together with those ladies whose husbands were to take part in the contest.

Now, the officers having gone about to measure distances and to see all set fair, the trumpets sang and the King-at-arms declared the tourney opened, 'in honour of the joyous advent of the Queen to Paris, by the most high and puissant prince Duke Francis of Valois and Bretagne'.

At that the new young Queen stood upright in her place;

and such was the effect of her bright beauty and the graciousness of her smiling, that the crowd roared their welcome and
for some time would not be stayed.

Now came the contestants to bow themselves before the
King and Queen. From the one side Duke Francis with the
Duke of Alençon, their knights behind them, all of them in
crimson and silver. About his arm Duke Francis wore the
Queen's own colours, white and green, which surprised her
without pleasure: she thought it overbold of him. But the old
King, delighted with the pretty compliment, clapped his thin
hands. From the other side rode the English challengers headed
by my lord of Suffolk and my lady of Dorset.

Now, followed by their knights, the contestants rode twice
about the lists, their shields and lances striking out light from
the winter sunshine. As they passed the King and Queen each
knight bowed his crested head so that the plumes lay upon
their horses' necks. Used to courtly behaviour though she was,
the sight of these proud plumes lowered in her honour touched
Mary to the quick of her heart; and seeing Brandon as he
passed, and knowing that he wore her riband close to his
heart, she breathed before she was aware of it a prayer for his
safety.

The lists were to last three days; from the beginning it
was clear that this was no mere joyous exhibition of skill but a
battle between English and French – a battle, if need be, to the
death. This first day consisted of fifteen courses with lances
only. Challengers and challenged sat their steeds face to face;
behind each rode one hundred and five knights, weapons
poised. Dorset and Alençon engaged one with the other,
fighting with great determination; behind them men fought
and several were slain – the bright blood gushed and made
slippery the grass as they were borne away. But it was clear
from the outset that it was between Suffolk and Duke Francis
that the issue lay. Watching these two fighting it would seem
to the death, Mary could not keep her seat but must stand
upright to watch every move, her heart and soul with Brandon.

And now, Alençon being unhorsed and Duke Francis

wounded in the hand, to fight no more that day nor on any other, the lists were closed; the English were judged the winners and Brandon, because he had broken more lances than any other, bore away the prize. Mary's heart rejoiced; hers was an English heart and, in spite of her will, a lover's heart.

The second day the challengers were Monsieur de Bourbon and the Duke of Lorraine. Again Suffolk so distinguished himself that even the French must stand up and cheer.

In his pavilion Duke Francis sulked. He had meant to show all Paris – and the Queen in particular – his grace, his skill and his prowess. Now, unable to hold either lance or sword, he was eaten with mortification, and with jealousy also. For the Queen, though she had thought to have given no sign, had, without knowing, clapped her hands together when Brandon made a skilful stroke, held her breath when he parried one.

The third day was yet to come, and the most dangerous. For now, not lances alone as on that first day, nor swords alone as on the second, but lances and sword both were to be used; a man would need eyes at the back of his head! For Brandon's honour Mary had no fear, but for his life she might well fear and – though she knew it not – with especial reason.

On this third day appeared a new contestant, a giant of a man, his arms unknown. Now my lord of Suffolk, who for two long days had fought valiantly, must fight to the uttermost of his strength and skill against the newcomer. Duke Francis, sitting by the King, smiled in his beard. After an equal bout of cut and thrust, Suffolk, in spite of his lesser stature, struck his opponent with the butt of his spear to send the giant staggering against the barriers. At that a cheer went up from French and English alike, for though Suffolk was a goodly man, the unknown was a Goliath and the odds were very great.

Mary stood, hand pressed to her heart, and Duke Francis stopped smiling.

The giant rose and, being unhorsed, must needs fight afoot. But, although under no obligation to do so, Suffolk dismounted; and such an act of chivalry gave rise to full-throated approval, and desire, even in French hearts, that so gallant a knight should win.

Now followed such a fight – such a game of cut and thrust if game it was – such swift and deadly sword-play that Mary hid her eyes and dared not look. The unknown had greater height and greater weight, Suffolk was swifter and nimbler, and had greater skill and grace. So, even now, no man could say how the contest might go. Behind her closed eyes, Mary prayed; the old King rose from his couch and stood, both hands clutching the rail of the royal enclosure; beside him stood Duke Francis, brows black and biting upon his lips. Into the darkness of her own making broke the thunder of applause; Mary forced herself to look. There upon the ground lay the Goliath. She saw the judges let down the rail between those two; heard Suffolk adjudged the winner. She saw the victor turn himself about, bow his crested head first to the King and then to herself, thereafter bowing left and right to the crowd that clamoured his praises. He and Dorset, being now unhelmed, came by the King's wish into the royal enclosure. The old man lay exhausted upon his couch; Duke Francis had disappeared.

'My lords,' said the Queen, 'the King asks me to say how greatly you two have honoured your country in these three days and especially on this third day. He and I together rejoice that the prizes shall be carried into England. They shall be presented to you in full court on Sunday. The King would have spoken with you himself, but alas, my lords, you see he is sick.'

Suffolk bowed low; seeing her there, beautiful and loving and proud of his prowess, he feared lest he show his secret heart. For by now passion in him burned steady. He was head over heels in love. So Dorset, speaking for them both, said, 'It is the Queen's grace that honours England this day, for she is all goodness and wisdom – a joy to the King, his Council and all France.'

On the Sunday the King held a great banquet for Suffolk

and Dorset since they were to return home on the morrow; and, the feast being over, the Queen stood up in her place and with her own hands put about their necks the prizes, which were great chains of gold with a raised portrait of the King upon one side, and of the Queen upon the other. And to these the King added further gifts as a mark of his friendship.

If Suffolk and Dorset had brought honour to England, Duke Francis had brought shame upon himself and France. For, the ambassadors being gone, out came the truth. He had deceived everyone. The giant, the unknown champion, was a common soldier who, bearing no arms, had no right to fight in the tourney. Duke Francis had offended against the first law of chivalry. By the Queen's wish the matter was kept quiet; the King was a sick man and she would not have him troubled. But meeting the Duke, she said, 'You wore my colours without my leave and you dishonoured them.'

The red came up into his face as he answered, 'Madam the Queen, I have shamed not your colours but myself, myself only. If I may at any time atone, in any way serve you, that thing I will do even if it be to my own hurt. Before God I swear it!'

And seeing him so ashamed and so earnest she said, 'My lord, let us put the matter by!' But for all that she could not but wonder whether a man, devious in this matter, could prove devious in another if it prove to his convenience.

In spite of the feast and festival, in spite of her joy at seeing Brandon and her grief at his departure, Mary's mind had been much upon her brother's wife. Catherine had expected her child this month. The news came at last: ill news, the worst. Catherine had once again given birth to a dead child, and that child a son. Henry needed a child – a son to make his throne secure. He was but of the second generation of Tudor kings, second generation from civil war. And his was neither a faithful nor a gentle heart. He had already taken several women to his bed.

Mary kept her sorrows locked in her own heart. There were continual occasions in her honour – festivities, gifts and addresses to be received, public prayers to attend. And as the King, fading daily, had been carried to St Germain-en-Laye to rest, she must face these occasions alone. The ordeal she most dreaded was the reception of the chief members of the University of Paris.

'How can I receive such learned gentlemen?' she asked Duke Francis. 'Kings, princes and ambassadors I know how to receive. But scholars such as these! I cannot do it.'

'You shall do it with your accustomed grace,' he told her, his eyes greedy upon her.

She stood by the throne to receive the long procession robed all in black or scarlet. The foremost of them all bore in his hands a jewelled crown; it was garlanded with fresh flowers – three red roses, three white, and three lilies.

'Madam Queen,' he said, presenting it upon his knees, 'these roses were gathered in an English garden, plucked in the bud and preserved for this day. The first red rose stands for the Queen's beauty which is the admiration of all France, the second for the Queen's modesty and sweet friendliness. The third, which observe, Madam, bears three buds, stands for the Queen's humility, piety and devotion to God, which, she being so young, must grow with her years. The first of the three white roses shows the ancient royalty of the Queen's lineage, the second the fame of your country in the learned arts, and the third represents the fruitfulness of England, which fruitfulness we pray with God's grace shall prove itself in the person of the Queen.

'Now, Madam, for the lilies. They are the lilies of France; they signify the King's love for the Queen, his mercy to his people and his own sovereignty.'

By now she had lost the thread of the long and flowery speech. Duke Francis told her afterwards, 'Madam, he said you were like the young virgin they put into King David's bed when he was old. They compared you also with the Virgin Spouse of God – and truly, a virgin you will remain unless

God Himself move in the matter, or unless He appoint a deputy!' And his eyes were bold.

'My lord,' she said, 'I pray to that same God you so lightly mention that I mistake your meaning.'

'They ended,' he continued, ignoring her words, 'by promising especial loving prayers for your fruitfulness' – and again his eyes mocked – 'and everything of love and joy such prayers must bring.'

'Sir,' she told him, 'this is no time for such love and joy as they have in mind. I am troubled about the King, and I am weary to death of these occasions. We are but fourteen miles from St Germain; the King will wish to know of today's happenings; I shall join him at once.'

'Not now,' he entreated. 'It is late. Leave it until tomorrow; we can set out as early as the Queen pleases. But to ride in the dark of a winter's night, and the Queen so weary – the King would not expect it.'

'He does not expect it, gentle and thoughtful as he is. But it will give him pleasure, the greater because unexpected. As for me, I am weary of the stale air of so many people; the night breeze shall carry it all away.'

She did not add her true reason. She had no desire to be left with the Duke, lacking the King's protection. Should the King die and Francis offer to make her his Queen, it could be done without much difficulty. The old King had shown the way, divorcing his first wife to gain Brittany with his second. She had no desire for a continuing crown; and had she the desire she could not so wrong the gentle Claude. And, above all, she had but one true love . . . if God send him true!

Louise, Duchess of Savoy, also watched troubled. She knew her son. When Francis wanted a thing, that thing he meant to have whatever the cost. Soon the old King must die; Francis, clearly dazzled, might take it into his head to divorce Claude to marry this young Queen. And what would he get with her but bad debts? Besides, putting away Claude, he would lose Brittany – and that must not, could not be!

Claude herself was untroubled on this score. Had she been

a beauty she might have been jealous, but she knew her steady calming influence on her husband. She was dutiful and she carried his heir. She never interfered with, or showed knowledge even of his light pleasures – and he had women aplenty. Passionate he was, but full of good sense. He knew very well his passions did not last. To marry Mary, were she a widow, would cost him too much to gain too little.

He and Mary rode out in the clear dark night, the sky bright with stars, the darkness lit by flaming torches. The last mile or so up to the castle she was glad to take to the litter, for by now she was bone-weary.

Having refreshed her person and eaten a little she went with Duke Francis to the King's bedchamber. She found him flushed and feverish, overcome with joy and astonishment that she should have braved the cold and dark for his sake. She told him of this day's audience, the Duke interrupting with his praises. 'Sir, Madam the Queen does not do herself justice. She does not speak of the sweet grace nor yet of the patience with which she received so tedious an embassy. She is, sir, the eighth wonder of the world.'

The King was clearly slipping from life, and it seemed to her not too much to make his last days as happy as might be. He seemed never content unless she were at his side. She would sing him little songs, herself plucking upon the lute; or, if he were well enough, he would tell her of his own young days, long before her own eyes had opened upon the world. These days she might have had from him whatever she desired, even the crown jewels themselves. She asked nothing but to make the King's last days happy and then – back to her own country and to her love. Affection for her husband she had, but it was a daughter's affection; how should she forget the promise her brother had made before she left for France – a promise she had thrust from her mind until the time should come to redeem it? She could now no longer forget it.

It was mid-December when they returned to Paris; the King was so frail they feared he could not stand the journey. But *Paris, Paris, Paris* . . . he had said it over and over again;

and, though she doubted the wisdom of it, fearing he should die on the way, Duke Francis said, 'His days are numbered. One day more or less, what does it matter so he have his heart's wish? To Paris he shall go!' And already he spoke with the authority of a king.

So the procession, subdued as a funeral train, made its slow way to Paris. She would always remember how, as the litter reached the bottom of the hill, the King had bade them stop; he had asked to be lifted high upon his pillows so that he might see the palace dark upon the summit, and the river winding its slow way among the water-meadows. 'We shall come back in the spring,' he told Mary; but for him there would be no spring.

They were back at the Tournelles Palace where they found a letter from Henry thanking the old King for his goodness to the Queen. And Louis, his eyes already dimming, his hand shaking, wrote his answer.

. . . I understand the pleasure you have to hear of my joy in the Queen, my wife, your dear sister. She has always carried herself towards me, and so does every day, in such a way that I cannot but be delighted with her. I love and honour her more every day . . .

It was written but three days before his death; the last letter he ever wrote.

New Year's Day came in. A bad, wet day, very cold. The old King had lain quiet, sleeping. He stirred and put out a blind hand towards the place where Mary sat; she took it gently within her own. He sighed very deep and so was gone.

She was sitting, the dead hand still in hers, whispering a prayer for his soul when there came to her Madam Claude who was now Queen.

'Madam,' she said, bending the knee as though she were still the Princess only, 'they are making ready for the Queen's retirement. The Cluny Palace is the accustomed place; will it suit the Queen?'

'It will do well enough.' Mary knew the French custom. A widowed Queen must keep her room for six full weeks, windows darkened that no daylight enter. She holds no court, and receives no visits save from women only; she sees no man ever, unless it be the new King or her own confessor. She wears white only, and indeed is supposed to spend the long and weary days in bed.

The next day she was borne in a coach hung all with black; behind her rode her ladies, clad in black, upon black horses and leading them all the Duchess Louise, mother to Francis who was now King, but must not as yet be so named. And as the mourning coaches passed, the people stood bareheaded in the bitter cold remembering the young Queen who had so lately come among them – a golden Queen in a golden coach, who now rode black-clad in a coach of sable.

And she, driving through the pale sunshine, thought with a sinking heart that for forty-two days she would see neither sky nor sun nor even the bare branches moving against the winter sky . . . and that the old man who had been her husband would see them never again.

In the mourning-chamber they undressed the Queen and put on her a shift of white linen and upon that a bedgown of white; for until the days of mourning were ended she must not be dressed. There, in the loose white robe in the white-hung chamber, lit only by tall wax candles burning so still they seemed pictured rather than real, she might herself be a ghost. Yet it was a very handsome apartment. The hangings were of white silk; the bed of State in which she had comforted her husband's old age, her virginity never broken, awaited her. But the white bedcurtains were not those she remembered, nor was the white fur bedcover. To right and left of the bed stood, as always, its two familiar statues – two knights fully accoutred, carrying the one his sword, the other his spear, as though to protect the sleepers. The room was heavy with the scent of those lilies that the reverend Master of Paris University had said signified the love of the old King for his wife; Duke Francis had sent them. He had sent also a chess-table, checkered in amber and crystal, with the pieces to match, saying that he trusted the pretty toy would a little distract her from her grief.

In the Tournelles Palace the dead King lay in state. Day and night the high peers of France kept unceasing vigil, and all day long the people passed weeping. His face had lost something of its weakness; in the carven dignity of death, he looked what he had been – the father of his people.

On the tenth day of January, the coffin was closed and covered with a rich black pall bearing his arms set within a border of *fleurs-de-lys* stitched in gold. A great black procession began to wind its way through the streets hung with black where the mourning crowds waited, every man among them clad in black or with a twist of black upon his arm. First came the priests chanting, bishops with censers swung before them, and high officers of the household. Immediately before the funeral carriage, drawn by horses trapped in the same sable colour, rode the ladies of the court, heavily veiled, headed by Queen Claude. Within the carriage, upon the pall, lay the King's effigy carved in wood, painted in life-like colour, robed and crowned. Behind it walked peers, knights and ambassadors clad top-to-toe in black. And, as the old King passed on his last journey, there went from the people a deep long sigh; and women and even men openly wept.

And so the procession took its sad slow way to Notre Dame, while within the white chamber, the white Queen sat and mourned.